Transatlantic Tragedy
Cruise Ship Cozy Mystery Series
Book 16

Hope Callaghan

hopecallaghan.com

Visit my website for new releases and special offers: hopecallaghan.com

Thank you to these wonderful ladies who help make my books shine - Peggy H., Cindi G., Jean P., Wanda D., Barbara W., Renate P. and Alix C. for taking the time to preview *Transatlantic Tragedy,* for the extra sets of eyes and for catching all of my mistakes.

A special THANKS to my reader review team:

Alice, Alta, Amary, Becky, Brinda, Carolyn, Cassie, Charlene, Christina, Debbie, Denota, Devan, Diann, Grace, Jan, Jo-Ann, Joyce, Jean K., Jean M., Judith, Katherine, Lynne, Megan, Melda, Kat, Linda, Lynne, Pat, Patsy, Paula, Rebecca, Rita, Theresa, Valerie, Vicki.

i

Contents

Cast of Characters

Mildred "Millie" Sanders-Armati. Millie, heartbroken after her husband left her for one of his clients, decides to take a position as assistant cruise director aboard the mega cruise ship, Siren of the Seas. From day one, she discovers she has a knack for solving mysteries, which is a good thing since some sort of crime is always being committed on the high seas.

Annette Delacroix. Director of Food and Beverage on board Siren of the Seas, Annette has a secret past and is the perfect accomplice in Millie's investigations. Annette is the "Jill of all Trades" and isn't afraid to roll up her sleeves and help out a friend in need.

Catherine "Cat" Wellington. Cat is the most cautious of the group of friends and prefers to help Millie from the sidelines, but when push comes to shove, Millie can count on Cat to risk life and limb in the pursuit of justice.

Danielle Kneldon. Millie's previous cabin mate. Headstrong and gung ho, Danielle loves a good adventure and loves physical challenges, including scaling the side of the ship, scouring the jungles of Central America and working undercover to solve a mystery.

Chapter 1

Millie Armati stood at the balcony railing; the blaring horns of the stevedores as they sped back and forth on their forklifts caught her attention.

The cruise ship's loading area had been a beehive of activity since Siren of the Seas had docked in the Port of Miami to drop off the last batch of sunburned vacationers returning from their seven-day Southern Caribbean cruise.

Soon, a new wave of passengers would begin boarding and Millie, along with Andy Walker, the ship's cruise director, would be on hand to greet them to begin their long journey across the Atlantic Ocean.

Millie had heard the passengers who were departing...the families with young children, career-minded professionals, and large groups of extended families taking their weeklong break on board the ship was a much different crowd than those who would soon join them.

According to both Nic, Millie's husband, and Andy, her boss, the new group would consist mostly of well-seasoned travelers, many already retired and enjoying their golden years, those who had both the means and the time to enjoy the lengthy cruise from Miami to Southampton.

"You're still here?" Nic, the ship's captain, stepped behind his wife and slipped his arms around her waist. "I thought you would be upstairs grabbing a bite to eat."

"I'm not hungry."

Nic gave his wife a quick hug before loosening his grip. "It's time to stop stressing out about the voyage and embrace it as a new adventure."

"I keep reminding myself, but you know how I feel." Ever since Millie found out the ship was repositioning from the Caribbean to the British Isles for the upcoming summer season, she'd teetered between excitement at the prospect of visiting other countries to sheer terror at being thousands of miles from home...and family.

Not only were they embarking on a summer season across the pond, but Nic was also working on carving out some time off to take Millie to his childhood home in the small village of Bertoli.

Before departure, Nic and Millie had traveled to Michigan to visit her children and grandchildren. It was a bittersweet visit, and the thought of it made her want to burst into tears.

"How...many days are we going to be at sea?" Another concern at the top of Millie's long list was how she would handle the motion of the ship, not to mention the endless sea days.

"We'll be traveling for thirteen days." Nic's radio blared, and Millie recognized Staff Captain Vitale's clipped voice, barking orders to the crewmembers working on the loading dock.

"Our maintenance crew and the delivery drivers are at each other's throats."

"I'm sure storage is a concern. It will be tight quarters stocking enough food for almost two weeks," Millie said.

"We will be stopping in Bermuda and the Azores," Nic reminded her. "The stops will help break up the long voyage, and we'll be able to pick up any extra supplies if necessary."

His radio went off again, and this time there was a hint of desperation in Vitale's voice. "If Sharky doesn't watch it, he's not going to make it to Southampton."

"You better get out of here," Millie chuckled.

Sharky, the ship's dayshift maintenance supervisor, could be a handful at times, but she sympathized with the fact his job was more than a little stressful, especially on changeover days as they offloaded the previous week's provisions and waste

4

and then loaded the supplies needed for the long voyage, all within a matter of hours.

Nic made his way out while Millie coaxed Scout, their teacup Yorkie, back inside the apartment. She trailed behind her husband before heading to the ship's gangway to check on Andy who was seeing the last few passengers off.

"Have we finished clearing the ship?"

"Barely." He pulled a handkerchief from his pocket and patted his forehead. "I thought I was going to have to personally escort the last few guests off."

"The passengers had so much fun, they're reluctant to leave," Millie said.

"It's a good problem to have." Andy consulted his watch. "I'm heading to my office. The important delivery I've been waiting for is finally here."

"The surprise."

Andy had been talking about a special surprise he'd purchased for the entertainment staff for weeks now. His plan was to "roll it out" during the repositioning cruise. So far, he'd refused to give even the tiniest hint at what it was, which concerned Millie.

Andy and surprises were never a good combination.

"I can hardly wait. I'm guessing it has something to do with the entertainment schedule."

"You could say that." Andy rubbed his hands together. "If this works half as good as I think it will, it's going to transform the way we entertain, make us leaner, more productive and put us at the top of our game."

"Speaking of entertaining, what if we can't keep the passengers entertained for days on end?"

"You worry too much. These repositioning cruisers...they're different than the weeklong cruisers. They'll quickly settle into their daily routines. You'll hardly know they're on board."

"I like to stay busy," Millie said. "Interacting with the passengers is what makes it exciting."

"You'll be fine. Mark my words." Andy reminded Millie to join him again in about an hour and then excused himself to check out his "special surprise."

After he left, Millie wandered upstairs to say "hello" to her friend, Cat, but the gift shop was dark and empty. She continued to the galley and eased the door open. Annette Delacroix, another of Millie's close friends, was off to the side conducting a staff meeting.

Not wanting to interrupt, she'd gone back downstairs to the main atrium to wait for Andy when she spied a man dressed in tails, a top hat and carrying a cane. He stood near the gangway chatting with Suharto, or more like arguing judging by the aggravated expression on the security employee's face.

A petite young woman with sandy brown hair was standing next to him. He began motioning wildly, and Millie made her way over. "Is there a problem?"

The man, his back ramrod straight, slowly turned. He clicked the tip of his cane on the gleaming marble floor. "This crewmember is unable to find me or my assistant on the employee roster."

He reached into his jacket pocket, pulled out a card and handed it to Millie. "Allow me to introduce myself. I'm Blackjack Blaze, the jack of all trades, at your service."

Millie glanced at the front of the card, "Blackjack Entertainment Services." Below his name was a telephone number. She flipped it over. "Magic tricks, comedy routines, ventriloquism."

Her eyes narrowed as she struggled to read the smaller print at the bottom. "Pest control, house painting and snow removal."

"As I said, I'm the jack of all trades. The other helps pay the bills in between gigs." Blackjack extended his hand. "And you are?"

"Millie Armati, Assistant Cruise Director."

"Assistance... Yes, that is what we need. I would appreciate it if you could be of some assistance. I asked to speak with Mr. Walker, but he seems to be MIA."

Millie had heard Andy mention the new entertainer in passing. She turned to Suharto. "Mr. Blaze is joining the entertainment staff for this voyage. He'll be with us until we reach Southampton."

"Correct," the man said. "I had hoped Mr. Walker, an acquaintance of mine, would be on hand to show us to our accommodations and give us a tour of the ship."

"You don't have a keycard?" Millie asked.

"No. There was some sort of mix-up. Andy informed me the keycards would be waiting for us inside our cabins."

"I see." Millie smiled at the young woman. "You're working on board as well?"

"Yes. I'm Wendy Rainwell, Blackjack's assistant."

"It's nice to meet you, Wendy." Millie shook her hand. "I'll show you to the crew quarters first, so you can drop off your bags."

Blackjack studied the small slip of paper he was holding. "Wendy is in C110. I'm down the hall in C112."

The trio descended the aft stairs and stepped into the long corridor, nicknamed "I95" by the crew. It ran the length of the ship and was wide enough for two forklifts to pass each other going in opposite directions.

They turned off the main corridor and onto a narrower side corridor. Millie stopped in front of

10

C112. "This is your cabin. Wendy's cabin is next to yours."

She slipped her keycard in the slot and opened the door. "The light switch is on the right."

Blackjack flipped the light on and took a tentative step inside. "This...is it?"

Millie peeked around the corner. "Yes. Although the accommodations for staff and crew are basic, you'll find you have everything you need."

Blackjack steered his luggage over the threshold. "Where's the window?"

"There are no windows. I take it you've never worked on a cruise ship before."

"I have. We recently completed a contract with Exotic Voyages Cruise Lines. This cabin is shabby and cramped compared to my previous accommodations."

Millie didn't know what to say. Having never seen another cruise ship's crew cabins, she had nothing to compare it to. "I'm sorry. Perhaps you can talk to Andy about moving to a different cabin."

Wendy studied Millie's nametag while Blackjack explored his accommodations. "Millie Armati, Assistant Cruise Director." Her eyes widened. "You're the captain's wife."

"I am." Before Millie could elaborate, Andy appeared, and Blackjack joined them.

"Blackjack Blaze." Andy let out a hearty laugh and whacked the man on the back. "Glad you could make it."

"I'm not sure if I'm glad. This cabin is ridiculously cramped."

"I tried to squeeze you into a bigger one, but the ship is at capacity. Since we brought you on last minute, it's all we had available. I hope it'll do. Did you find your keycard? I left it on the nightstand." Andy ignored the frown on the man's face and turned to Wendy. "You must be Blackjack's assistant."

"Yes. I'm Wendy Rainwell." She shook Andy's hand. "I'm sure my cabin will be fine. Besides, I don't plan on spending a lot of time in it."

"No, you won't." Andy motioned to Millie. "Suharto told me you rescued Blaze. I can take over from here. There's just enough time for me to give Blackjack and Wendy a quick tour before the passengers begin arriving."

"I'll open Wendy's cabin door so she can drop her things off." Millie hurried ahead, and swiped her card before stepping to the side.

"Thanks." The young woman disappeared inside her cabin, returning moments later, keycard in hand. "I found mine."

"Perfect. Enjoy your tour with Andy." Millie turned to go when the clatter of heavy footsteps rumbled behind her. She stumbled backward to get out of the way as several crewmembers ran past, a frantic look on their faces.

Annette wasn't far behind them. She barreled around the corner nearly colliding head-on with Millie. "Sorry, Millie."

"What's going on? Is the ship on fire?"

"No. It's Sharky. There's a big problem down on the loading dock."

Chapter 2

"Sharky's gone off the deep end." Annette grabbed Millie's hand and dragged her down the hall. "There's a standoff between him, Joe, our beverage manager, and the stevedores. The port authorities are threatening to call the cops and your husband is trying to intervene."

The women ran to the other end of the hall and descended the steps. They reached the maintenance deck at the same time two other maintenance employees ran past.

"Follow them." Annette and Millie picked up the pace as they jogged to the other end of the ship and the open doorway.

A group of stevedores had gathered in a semi-circle surrounding Sharky, along with Nic and Donovan Sweeney, the ship's purser.

"I got a full ship." Sharky, his face beet red, pointed at the gangway. "The only room we have left for these last loads is on the other end."

One of the stevedores, the one closest to the gangway, hopped off his forklift. "And I told you...I can't put these loads at the other end. My manifest says we have to load in zone two." He jabbed his finger at the marking above the gangway. "This is zone two. Last time you asked me to move a load; I got chewed out."

Nic attempted to smooth things over as he pulled his cell phone from his pocket. "I can call the dock manager to get your instructions changed. We need the loads, but as our maintenance supervisor pointed out, we're out of room."

"I don't have time for this." The man stomped back to his forklift and climbed onto the seat. "We'll put these last few loads back in the building, and you can figure it out on your own."

From her vantage point, Millie could see the veins in Sharky's neck bulge. "Wait a coupla minutes and you'll have the approval."

"There's a new problem with you every week, Sharky. I'm sick and tired of it." The man fired up the forklift and reached for the lever.

"I'll give you something to get sick and tired of." Sharky took a step forward.

"Stay back," the stevedore warned.

"I'll make sure you never work another day on this dock," Sharky took another menacing step.

"That's it." The stevedore released the load of boxes on the front of the forklift. They hit the concrete with a loud crash and the ear-splitting sound of breaking glass.

Amber liquid poured out of the broken boxes, and the overwhelming stench of sugary root beer filled the air.

Things moved fast after that. Sharky's stocky legs covered the ground quickly. He scrambled onto the forklift and took a swing at the stevedore.

Two of the ship's security guards sprang into action and quickly ended the scuffle, pulling Sharky off the forklift and dragging him back toward the ship.

A Miami-Dade patrol car, along with another port authority vehicle, arrived moments later and Millie wondered if they would arrest Sharky.

Nic lifted both hands as he stepped between Sharky and the authorities. Unfortunately, Millie was too far away to hear what he was saying. Finally, the uniformed port authority released his grip, and she let out the breath she was holding.

Nic and Donovan Sweeney approached the other stevedores whose forklifts were loaded with towering stacks of the same brown boxes.

After a brief discussion between the stevedores, they began driving to the other loading ramp and one by one, making their way onto the ship while Nic and Donovan escorted Sharky back on board.

The other crewmembers hurriedly cleared the area, leaving only Millie, Annette and Reef, the other maintenance supervisor, standing near the gangway.

"I'm sorry, boss man. I got fed up with that joker. He's always giving me a hard time." Sharky motioned to the dock, now littered with ripped boxes and broken bottles. "You saw what he did."

"You didn't have to take a swing at him." Donovan placed a light hand on Sharky's shoulder. "I know you're having a rough day, but losing a whole load of beverages will have to be reported to corporate."

"I'm not the one who dumped them." Sharky's shoulders sagged. "You gonna write me up?"

"Not this time. The port will have to reimburse us for the damaged goods."

Reef joined the men. "I can finish getting the rest of the loads on board."

"Thanks, Reef," Donovan said. "I think it's best if Sharky steers clear of the stevedores for the rest of the day."

Reef, along with Annette and Millie, waited until Donovan, Nic and Sharky were out of sight. *"Ninety-nine bottles of root beer on the lift, ninety-nine bottles of root beer...break them all because of a brawl...zero bottles of root beer on the lift."*

"Poor Sharky," Millie grimaced.

Annette shook her head. "He needs to learn to control his temper."

"You could help him with his anger issues," Millie teased.

"No thanks. I have enough on my plate without having to worry about that hot-headed mess."

"It was a close one. I'm glad the boss man cut Sharky some slack. I better get back to work." Reef hurried down the ramp to finish directing the stevedores while Millie and Annette returned upstairs.

Millie's friend stopped her when they reached the upper decks. "I have something for you."

"For me?"

"It's a surprise. You got a minute? It's in the galley."

"Sure."

When the women reached the galley, Annette grabbed a large Ziploc baggie filled with a thick brown substance off the counter and handed it to Millie.

"What's this?"

"Friendship bread."

"Friendship bread?" Millie lifted the bag to inspect the contents. "Never heard of it."

"I was searching through some old recipes the other day and found it. This is your batch. Both sets of instructions are taped to the back."

"Ah, I know what this is." Millie flipped the bag over, her eyes skimming the top sheet. "This is the recipe you gotta babysit."

"Not babysit. Nurture...you're nurturing it."

"Fine. Nurturing. I'm not good at this stuff. Hopefully, you're not using this batch as an experiment."

"Nah." Annette waved dismissively. "It's just for fun. I made a batch for Cat, Danielle, Amit and Andy, too."

Millie chuckled. "What did Andy say?"

"I haven't given him his yet."

Millie thanked her friend for the starter bread and made a quick trip home to drop it off. She set it on the counter and returned to the atrium to join Andy and greet the new arrivals.

The first wave of guests, the diamond passengers, descended on them. There were several familiar faces in the crowd and Millie greeted them by name.

A second wave of passengers followed behind, all in high spirits and ready for the long voyage.

Another familiar face emerged from the crowd and the man made his way over. "Millie Sanders-Armati." The man's hazel eyes twinkled with mischief as he reached for her hand and gently kissed the top. "We meet again."

"Thomas Windsor. You're cruising with us?"

"I had so much fun on my last cruise, I figured I would give a transatlantic trip a try."

"It will be my first, too," she whispered confidentially. "We're both in the same boat."

"Or on the same ship," he quipped. "I managed to snag an amazing last minute deal on an inside cabin."

"The ladies will be thrilled to have you on board. We have an exciting couple of weeks planned."

"And I look forward to every second of it."

Andy caught the last of their exchange. "You remember Mr. Windsor?"

"Of course. The female passengers will be vying for the 'Silver Fox's' attention. He should liven things up with the women who are cruising with us."

Thomas rolled his eyes. "I don't know where I got that nickname."

Millie pointed to the man's silver locks. "Silver locks on the Silver Fox."

He cast a quick glance over Millie's shoulder and then ducked down. "I hate to cut our reunion short, but I see Lenore Bernitz headed our way." Windsor fumbled for the handle of his carry-on. "This is my cue to exit the area."

"Already dodging the ladies." Millie laughed as he dashed toward the bank of elevators.

Andy watched him slip into the crowd. "I don't know how he does it. Maybe he could give me some pointers."

It took another couple of hours for the steady stream of passengers to die down. Finally, Suharto gave his men the signal to remove the gangway.

Millie zigzagged past a cluster of lounge chairs, peering out the large picture window as the ship glided effortlessly out of Biscayne Bay, between Fisher Island on one side and South Beach on the other. She watched South Beach become smaller and smaller - until it was a tiny dot of sand off in the distance.

"We're on our way."

Millie clutched her chest and spun around to find Danielle, another member of the entertainment staff, standing directly behind her. "You scared me."

"Sorry. I thought you saw me coming."

"I was too busy saying good-bye to home, although it does help knowing Beth and the family will be joining us in a couple of months." Nic had pulled some strings and booked a cabin for Millie's daughter, her daughter's husband and grandchildren for one of their twelve-day British Isles cruises.

The overhead horn blared, followed by a recording that announced the beginning of the safety drill.

"That's our signal. See you later." Danielle gave Millie a quick wave and darted off.

The muster drill dragged on for what seemed like forever, with the staff repeatedly announcing several names over the intercom. Finally, the mandatory drill ended and the rest of the afternoon passed quickly as the passengers settled in.

During her late afternoon break, Millie ran up to the buffet to grab a quick bite to eat before beginning a round of "Everything Bermuda" trivia.

Bermuda was their first port stop, and although she didn't plan to leave the ship, Millie hoped on their return trip to Miami in the fall, Nic and she would have some free time to see the sights.

The trivia ended, and the bars on board began setting up for live music. There was a swing band, a jazz ensemble, and a toe-tapping country music trio.

Millie finished checking on the entertainers and headed to Andy's office. She started to knock but stopped when she heard his booming voice.

"...you should have told me this before the ship departed Miami."

Millie could tell from the tone of her boss's voice that he was annoyed.

"I had no idea. She didn't tell me until the ship left the port." Millie recognized the second voice. It was the new entertainer, Blackjack Blaze.

"This is certain to cause complications," Andy said. "Perhaps it would have been best if you had hired a different assistant before accepting this position."

Through the crack in the door, Millie watched as Andy began to pace. "You said she hinted the baby's father is a Siren of the Seas kitchen crewmember?"

"Yes, but she's not divulging his name. She claims she's afraid he'll lose his job. The only thing I know is she met the man at Azure. It's a club not far from the Bayfront area."

"I'll need to tell Captain Armati. We don't need this sort of drama."

Millie slowly backed away from the door. Wendy, Blaze's assistant, was pregnant and the baby belonged to someone who worked in Annette's kitchen. She must not have been very far along since she wasn't showing.

Why didn't the woman track the man down when they were in port? Unless he was avoiding her, not to mention the fact they were leaving for the season and wouldn't return to Miami until fall. Andy was right…the predicament could lead to some unwanted drama. The fact they were traveling for days at sea could be a major problem.

She wandered around the dressing area until she heard the sound of heavy steps on the stage floor. Blackjack had left. She waited a few more minutes and then returned to Andy's office. He was alone and staring off into space.

"Hey, Andy."

"Hello, Millie." Andy attempted a smile. "How was your first official day of our transatlantic cruise?"

"Not bad." Millie sank down in the chair across from him. "So far, so good. How about you?" She wondered if Andy would mention Wendy and the baby.

"I've had better days."

"Your big surprise was a bust?"

"No. Have you ever heard the crewmembers mention Azure? It's a nightclub in Miami."

"I have. It's in Bayfront District, not far from the port. Isla has talked about it. I've never been there."

"We have a small issue...with the entertainment staff." Andy shifted his gaze, staring at her thoughtfully. "It involves our new entertainer, Blackjack Blaze, and his assistant, Wendy."

Andy briefly recapped his conversation with Blaze. "Wendy has so far refused to name the baby's father, who happens to be a kitchen crewmember. I was thinking if you chatted with her, woman-to-woman, she might confide in you."

"I...could try."

"Thanks, Millie. I knew I could count on you." Andy patted her hand. "She has the evening off. You could stop by her cabin under the premise of checking on her."

"I have a few spare minutes. I'll swing by there now." Millie grabbed her work schedule for the following day and exited Andy's office.

Wendy didn't answer her cabin door, so Millie continued to the crew galley and then to the crew lounge. The young woman was nowhere in sight.

Millie turned to go when she caught a glimpse of her inside the employee computer area, standing near the back.

She took a tentative step and then abruptly stopped. Her heart skipped a beat when she recognized the person Wendy was talking with.

Chapter 3

Amit and Wendy stood talking near the back of the computer station, a serious expression on their faces. Their voices were low, and all she could pick up was the word "baby" and "child support."

Millie tiptoed backward until she was out of sight, her mind whirling. Were Amit and Wendy an item?

All of the ship's employees were allowed time off, depending on their work schedules, and Miami was popular among the younger crewmembers. There were several hotspots...hangouts for the crew of not only Siren of the Seas, but other Miami-based cruise ships.

She thought of the blossoming romance between Carlah, who worked at the specialty coffee shop, and Amit. Was Amit seeing two women? Millie immediately dismissed the thought. He wasn't the type of man to toy with women. In fact, she was thrilled when she heard Amit and Carlah were dating.

She paused in the hallway, torn between reporting to Andy what she'd seen and overheard and keeping quiet. Millie decided to mull it over first.

*****

The Welcome Aboard Show was Andy's last event of the evening. Millie waited for the theater to clear before making her way to his office in the back. "Knock, knock."

Andy glanced up, peering at her over the top of his reading glasses. "Hello, Millie. Were you able to chat with Wendy?"

"No." Millie hovered in the doorway. "I tracked her down. She was talking to Amit." Before she could change her mind, she quickly blurted out what she'd overheard.

Andy tapped his pen on top of the desk, quietly listening. He waited until she finished. "Do you think it's possible he's the father of Wendy's baby?"

"Maybe. I mean, this is pure speculation."

"I see." Andy cleared his throat. "I'll address the matter with Amit and Wendy tomorrow. Thank you for reporting back to me."

"You're welcome." Millie turned to go.

"Wait." Andy motioned for her to remain. "I'm holding a meeting here tomorrow at four for the big reveal to show you my surprise. I've come up with a plan I would like to implement before rolling it out to the rest of the staff."

"A plan?"

"Yep," Andy beamed. "If this works half as good as I think it will, my entertainment staff will be running like a well-oiled piece of machinery in no time."

"I didn't know we had issues."

"We don't, but when I need to make schedule changes, this will help ensure I can implement those changes seamlessly." Andy droned on about reducing downtime, increasing productivity and enhancing the passengers' entertainment experience.

Millie's eyes started to glaze over and finally, Andy stopped. "Enough talk about it for now. I'll give you more details tomorrow at four."

"Great, I can hardly wait."

Millie took a quick glance at her schedule before hustling upstairs. She moved from event to event, finally finishing at midnight before wearily heading home.

The bridge was quiet, and the only sound was the soft hum of the center console computers. Nic and First Officer Craig McMasters stood near the wall of windows staring out into the dark seas. Nic gave his wife a quick smile. "You've finished for the day?"

"Yes. I have to be up and at 'em early tomorrow." Millie waved her schedule. "Andy has an action-packed, fun-filled day at sea on tap."

"I'm sure he has. I'll be home shortly."

"I'll be waiting." Millie stepped down the short hall connecting the bridge and their apartment. Scout stood near the door waiting to greet her. He let out a small yip and then pounced on her shoe.

"It was a long day, wasn't it?" She dropped her work schedule on the dining room table and kicked her shoes off before carrying the pup to the balcony.

A warm ocean breeze tugged at wisps of her hair. Millie patted them in place and leaned against the railing, peering down the side of the ship.

From her vantage point, she could see the long strands of twinkling lights on the lido deck. Millie shifted her gaze in the opposite direction, toward the front of the ship and stared at the dark horizon.

A lump formed in her throat as she thought about how every hour was putting even more distance between them and everything familiar.

She was still standing on the balcony when Nic joined her a short time later. They chatted about the upcoming sea day and the port stop in Bermuda.

"Today flew by." Millie stifled a yawn and covered her mouth. "Excuse me. I think it's time to hit the hay." She scooped Scout up before following Nic up the stairs to their loft bedroom. She started to close the door when she remembered Annette's friendship bread. "I'll be right back."

Millie darted down the stairs and into the kitchen. The Ziploc bag was on the counter right where she'd left it. She scanned the instructions before stirring the thick mixture and re-zipping the bag.

She took a quick glance at the "Final Baking Instructions" before placing it on top of the bag and returning to the bedroom.

"Did you forget something?" Nic asked.

"Annette gave me a batch of beginner friendship bread. I was checking on it."

Her husband patted his stomach. "Homemade bread sounds good."

"I left it on the counter. I'll take care of it later," Millie promised.

The couple took turns in the bathroom and by the time Millie emerged, Nic was already dozing.

She waited for Scout to take his spot at the top of her pillow. He circled several times before curling up in a ball.

"How would you like to be my sidekick tomorrow?" Millie whispered.

Scout pawed at her hair.

"I'll take that as a 'yes.'"

During her prayers, Millie thanked God for a loving husband, her second family and her friends

38

on board the ship. Her prayer ended with a request for safe travels across the Atlantic Ocean.

She switched her bedside lamp off, closed her eyes, and was out like a light.

*****

Bap...BAP...BAAAAP.

Millie bolted upright in bed. "What was that?"

"It's the ship's emergency signal." Nic flung the covers back and turned his radio on.

"Oscar, Oscar, Oscar!" Felippe, one of the security guard's, frantic voice blared over the radio. "Starboard side, deck twelve."

"Man overboard." Millie fumbled with the bedside lamp. "Someone's gone over the side of the ship."

Nic pulled on his pants and reached for his shirt as the ship shuddered, gently shaking their bed.

"We're stopping."

"To go back and search." Nic grabbed his shoes and ran out of the bedroom. Millie was right behind him. She followed him to the front door. "Be careful."

Nic gave his wife a grim nod before exiting the apartment, the door slamming behind him.

After he left, Millie did the first thing that came to mind. She bowed her head and prayed that whoever had gone over was still alive, the ship would find the person and the ship's crewmembers would be safe while performing a rescue.

She slowly walked over to the balcony door and stared out into the pitch-black night. Performing a successful MOB...man overboard rescue during the day was difficult. The chances of finding the person in the deep, dark waters in the middle of the night would be a daunting task, if not nearly impossible.

Knowing she wouldn't be able to sleep, Millie returned upstairs. She donned a pair of sweatpants and a sweatshirt before slipping on a pair of sandals on her way out of the apartment.

Nic and Craig McMasters stood on the outboard bridge wing facing the open ocean, their backs to her.

She didn't slow as she made her way off the bridge and up the stairs to the starboard side of deck twelve. Unsure exactly where the incident had occurred, Millie made her way midship and then aft to the tiki bar.

Crewmembers stood shoulder to shoulder at the railing, holding large flashlights and shining them into the water.

Millie could see the ship was making a slow turn and heading in the opposite direction. She cautiously approached Oscar, one of the ship's security guards. "What happened?"

"A passenger is claiming someone went over the side of the ship."

"Intentionally?"

"We're not sure yet." Oscar told Millie the bartender, Dario, remembered seeing two people standing near the railing. He wasn't positive but thought they may have been crewmembers. Moments later, a passenger ran onto the deck claiming someone had gone overboard.

"So perhaps no one went over," Millie said. "I mean if they didn't actually see the person go over."

"We're checking surveillance cameras now." Oscar pointed to a tall post and two cameras positioned near the top. "If someone went over in the vicinity the passenger claims, the cameras should have caught something."

Millie thanked him for the information and made her way to the other side where more security staff, including Dave Patterson, the ship's head of security, and two passengers, stood talking. Careful to stay out of the way, she eased in behind them.

"I remember two people standing right here in this spot," the man insisted. "One of them was definitely a crewmember and wearing some sort of uniform."

"Were they arguing?"

"I don't know. I walked past them on my way to the restroom. When I returned to the deck, this woman was screaming something about man overboard."

Patterson turned to the woman who appeared visibly shaken. "You saw something."

"Y-yes." The woman nodded. "I had gotten out of the pool and was drying off. I was standing near the railing, thinking how dark the skies were. I turned to go when I heard someone screaming. That's when I saw the person. It was right before they hit the water." The woman covered her face with her hands while Patterson attempted to comfort her. "I'm sorry."

Millie stepped closer. "Is there anything I can do to help?"

Patterson shifted to the side to make room for Millie. "Mrs. Junmar witnessed someone going overboard. Perhaps you could get her a glass of water."

"Of course. I'll be right back." Millie stepped over to the bar where she found Dario bartending. "I need a glass of water for the passenger who claims she watched someone go overboard."

"It is terrible." Dario shook his head. "They are searching the water, but it is very dark."

"What did you see?" Millie asked.

"I remember seeing two people near the railing, but I wasn't paying attention. Looking back, I wish I had."

"There are so many people on board; it's hard to keep track of everyone. Thanks for the water." She returned to the woman's side and handed her the glass.

"I don't want to keep you any longer Mrs. Junmar and..." Patterson turned to the man standing next to her.

"Bud Kemp."

"Mr. Kemp. Thank you for your time. I have your information if I need to follow up."

"Would you like me to accompany you back to your cabin?" Millie asked the woman.

The woman's hand trembled as she set the glass on a nearby table. "Yes. Please. I can't get the sound of the anguished scream out of my mind."

Millie placed a light arm around the woman's shoulders and led her away from the scene. "Hopefully, by the time you wake in the morning, there will have been a rescue."

"Do you think they'll find the person?" Mrs. Junmar slowed. "It's dark, and the ship went quite a ways before it was able to turn around."

"I don't know," Millie answered truthfully. "We can pray for a miracle."

"Yes. A miracle."

When they reached the woman's cabin, Millie waited for her to step inside.

"Thank you for walking me home."

"You're welcome. If you need anything at all, I'm Millie Armati, the assistant cruise director."

Mrs. Junmar squeezed her eyes shut and sucked in a ragged breath. "It was awful."

"Try not to dwell on it." Millie touched her arm. "You've done everything you could to help." She waited until the woman closed the door and then whispered a small prayer before returning upstairs.

The ship was moving at a snail's pace, and there were even more crewmembers on hand. She watched as the ship's crew lowered lifeboats into the water. The trio of rescue boats began circling, moving out with each pass.

Millie made her way to the other side of the ship. There were three more lifeboats in the water, each circling in the same pattern.

She stayed on deck for another long hour, watching as they frantically searched the dark waters. Millie could tell from the expressions on the faces of the search team, any hope of finding the person was growing dim.

Exhausted, Millie finally decided to return home. She stopped to check on Nic, who told her to go on ahead. "It doesn't look promising," he said grimly.

"I could tell from the looks on the crewmembers' faces when I left that the chances of finding the person are growing slimmer by the minute."

"It will take a miracle for the person to be rescued."

"And found alive," Millie added.

Nic merely nodded.

"I'm sorry." Millie made her way to the apartment. She let Scout out for a short break and could see bright lights continuing to scan the waters.

She offered up another prayer for a miracle before crawling back into bed. Millie pulled the covers to her chin and stared up at the ceiling. All she could think was how awful it would be to hit the water, to see the cruise ship steaming ahead and knowing you were all alone.

She slept fitfully and woke with Scout curled around the top of her head. Nic's side of the bed was still empty.

After showering and dressing, Millie stepped on the bridge. Nic was there, along with Staff Captain Antonio Vitale.

She took one look at her husband's face and knew there was no hope of rescue. "No sign of the man overboard?"

"It was a recovery." Nic and Vitale exchanged a quick glance.

"A recovery...so someone died?"

"They did, and we've positively identified the victim."

Chapter 4

Millie pressed a hand to her chest. "I had hoped the passengers were mistaken. Who was it?"

"A member of the entertainment staff, a woman who boarded the ship Saturday. You may not have met her yet," Nic said.

"It wasn't Wendy Rainwell, was it?"

"You had met her."

"Wendy is Blackjack Blaze's assistant." Millie's breath caught in her throat. "I only spoke with her briefly."

"Are you all right?" Nic reached for his wife's hand. "You're white as a ghost."

"I...I'll be fine. What happened?"

"We don't know yet." Nic told his wife one of the ship's cameras was able to capture a clear shot of

Wendy's face. "She moved away from the camera, and from what we surmise, she was talking with someone. Moments later, a passenger, Mrs. Junmar, reported hearing her scream."

"So someone was with Wendy moments before the fall."

"It appears to be the case. Donovan is meeting with crewmembers this morning to find out if anyone knew Ms. Rainwell."

Millie thought about the previous evening when she spotted Wendy and Amit talking.

"I recognize the look on your face," Nic said. "You know something."

"Maybe. I'm not sure. I saw Wendy talking to a crewmember last night near the breakroom."

"Who?" Vitale, who had so far remained silent, spoke.

"Amit. Amit Uddin. He works with Annette in the kitchen." Millie hurried on. "There's no way he pushed Wendy over the side of the ship."

"But they knew each other," Vitale said.

"I don't know. They were talking, and their conversation appeared serious. I didn't want to interrupt, so I left."

"Serious?" Nic lifted a brow. "You must tell Patterson."

"I will. I already mentioned it to Andy last night. This is awful."

"For everyone involved," Nic agreed. "McMasters will be here to relieve me soon. I'm heading home to get some rest."

Millie told her husband she would come back a little later to grab Scout and then stepped off the bridge. She was halfway to the security office when she changed her mind.

She promised her husband she would tell Patterson about Amit, but before doing that, she wanted to talk privately with Annette to give her friend a heads up.

Despite the early hour, the galley was already a beehive of activity. Annette was front and center at the counter surrounded by an array of mixing bowls.

Millie caught her eye and wandered over.

"You're up early."

"I couldn't sleep." Millie pointed to the mixing bowls. "Whatcha working on?"

"Another batch of friendship bread. This one is a quicker version for the passengers."

Millie snorted. "And you gave me the long version?"

"I gave you the friend version," Annette said. "You remembered to stir it, right?"

"I did. In fact, I'll stir it again when I stop back by the apartment to pick up Scout."

Annette reached for a wooden spoon. "I heard about the entertainer who went overboard last night."

"Nic has been up all night."

"I'll never understand why someone would want to kill themselves by jumping off the side of a cruise ship in the middle of the ocean and at night, no less."

Millie shifted her feet. "Nic said they believe someone was with her around the time she went overboard."

Annette stopped stirring. "So they think she was pushed over the side of the ship?"

"Maybe. I..." Millie glanced around the galley. "I need to talk to you in private."

"Let's head to my office." Annette dropped the spoon and led her friend to the dry goods pantry. She waited until they were inside. "What is it?"

"It's Amit," Millie said in a low voice. "I saw him talking with Wendy, the woman who went overboard, shortly before the incident. They were in the employee computer area having a conversation. From what I could tell, it looked serious."

"Do you have any idea what they were talking about?"

"Maybe." Millie twined her fingers together.

"What?"

"Wendy was pregnant. She told her boss, Blackjack, the father of her baby was one of the kitchen crewmembers on board the ship. She met him in Miami at one of the bars, a popular hangout. She planned to confront him. Andy asked me to track her down hoping she would confide in me and tell me the name of the baby's father. That's when I found Wendy talking to Amit."

"So they were talking? What were they saying?"

"I only caught a couple of words." Millie paused.

"And?"

"I heard the word 'baby' and 'child support.'"

Annette's jaw dropped. "You're telling me Amit was the baby's father?"

"I...don't know," Millie confessed. "All I know is what I overheard. I'm on my way to talk to Patterson."

"Amit would never kill anyone. He wouldn't hurt a fly."

"I know, but this doesn't look good." Millie briefly closed her eyes. "Why would they be talking?"

"Maybe he met Wendy in Miami, they were friends, and he was trying to help her track down the baby's father," Annette theorized.

"It could be. I hope you're right."

One of the kitchen crewmembers approached the doorway. "Miss Annette, we have a problem with one of the soups."

"I'll let you get back to work." Millie followed Annette out of the galley.

"Hey." Annette snatched a bag off the counter and handed it to her. "Can you drop this off at the gift shop for Cat? She forgot her friendship bread."

"Sure."

"Tell her she can start with day two today."

"Will do." Millie gave her friend a thumbs up and exited the galley.

Ocean Treasures, the ship's main gift shop, was busy. She caught a glimpse of her friend near the jewelry counter.

Millie wandered over and waited until Cat finished helping a customer. "Annette said you forgot your friendship bread. You can start with day two."

Cat took the bag. "I'm sure she gave you one, too."

"Yes, and I almost forgot to stir it last night. It's like babysitting."

"Babysitting bread," Cat quipped. Her expression sobered. "I heard about the entertainer who went overboard last night."

"What a terrible tragedy. They were able to find her, but it was too late."

"So sad," Cat said, "to end one's life like that."

"It is. I haven't heard the cause of death." Millie quickly decided not to mention Amit's possible involvement. "I can't stay. I still need to run a couple of errands before starting my shift."

"Thanks for the bread."

"You're welcome." Millie stepped out of the gift shop and slowly began making her way to the stairs. She wished she'd never spotted Wendy and Amit chatting. Perhaps it was an innocent conversation.

Perhaps Annette was right and Amit was trying to help Wendy find the father of her child since he worked in the kitchen.

Patterson's office light was on and the door ajar. Millie gave it a couple of quick raps before sticking her head around the corner.

"Hey, Millie."

"Hi, Patterson. You got a minute?"

"For you, I've got two." He motioned her inside. "Are you enjoying your transatlantic cruise so far?"

"I'm only one day in. The jury is still out," Millie joked.

"It'll go by quickly, and if we're lucky it will be smooth sailing."

"Smooth sailing except for last night's tragic incident. Nic told me it was a recovery. The woman died."

"She did. We're working on notifying Ms. Rainwell's family."

"Do you think she jumped?" Millie eased into the seat near the door.

"We're still investigating. We believe there may have been another crewmember in close proximity around the time of Ms. Rainwell's fall."

Millie shifted uneasily. "I have something to tell you."

"About Wendy Rainwell?"

"Yes. I'm not sure how much you've heard. She was pregnant and anxious to track down the man she believed was the baby's father...a crewmember on board our ship."

"I talked to Blackjack Blaze and Andy already," Patterson nodded. "We're questioning several crewmembers; anyone we think may have had contact with Rainwell last evening."

"I met her and Blackjack Blaze when they boarded. Andy explained what had happened, how Wendy confided in Blaze after they boarded the ship her plan to confront the baby's father. He asked me to try to talk to her, to head off potential drama."

Patterson leaned forward in his chair. "And?"

"I was able to track her down." Millie and Patterson's eyes met before she looked away.

"What is it, Millie?"

"She was talking with Amit Uddin, Annette's galley assistant."

"I heard. Wendy refused to name the baby's father, but told Blaze the man worked in the kitchen."

"I know," Millie answered in a small voice. "I also know Amit did not kill Wendy. I mean, they were just talking."

"Andy already mentioned Amit. I would like you to tell me exactly what you overheard."

Millie sucked in a breath, knowing what she was about to say would throw Amit right under the bus. "I heard the words 'baby' and 'child support.'"

Patterson slammed his palm on the office desk, and Millie jumped.

"Sorry."

"I know how this looks, how it sounds. I also know there's no way Amit would've intentionally pushed Wendy over the side of the ship. He doesn't have a mean bone in his body."

Patterson's voice tightened as he thanked Millie for the information. He abruptly stood, his signal he was ready for her to leave.

Sudden tears burned the back of Millie's eyes. Her friend was in deep trouble, and it was her fault. "Don't end your investigation with him. I think there's something more to Wendy's...death."

"I can see you're upset over what you told me, Millie. You did the right thing, no matter how hard it was," Patterson said kindly. "I promise the matter will be thoroughly investigated."

Millie knew it was the only promise she could expect out of Patterson. She slipped out of his office and slowly made her way upstairs to the buffet.

She grabbed an empty plate and began circling the food stations. The thought of eating after hearing about Wendy's death, not to mention Amit's involvement, made her stomach churn.

Millie forced herself to focus on food before finally settling on a half grapefruit, some scrambled eggs and a small stack of crispy bacon. She grabbed a cup of coffee and headed toward the back when she spied Danielle seated at a table near the window. "Mind if I join you?"

"Of course not." Danielle slid a set of silverware off to the side. "You look like you lost your best friend."

"I may have...at least one of them." Millie plopped down in the chair. "I'm sure you heard about Wendy Rainwell's death."

"It's all anyone is talking about. Rumor has it she jumped."

"It's possible." Millie changed the subject. "What's on your schedule for the day?"

"The usual...a cycling class, I'm hosting a bridge game along with lido deck games. I see that Andy added some extra activities to keep the passengers entertained."

Millie pulled her work schedule from her front pocket and unfolded it. "There's a port of call lecture for Bermuda, which sounds intriguing."

"Are you getting off in Bermuda?" Danielle reached for her apple and took a big bite.

"I don't think so. Nic and I have some time off together when we reach the Azores."

The topic drifted to Danielle's new roommate before returning to the entertainer's tragic fall overboard.

Millie finished her food first and stood. "I need to get going. Scout is waiting for me to pick him up." She dropped her dirty dishes in the bin by the door and returned to the bridge.

Craig McMasters was on hand, along with another crewmember Millie vaguely recognized. "Nic left to get some rest about an hour ago."

"Thanks for the heads up. I'll be sure to keep quiet." Millie swiped her keycard and eased their front door open.

Scout was nowhere in sight, and she could hear humming coming from the kitchen. Millie rounded the corner where she found her husband standing in front of the oven.

"What in the world?"

Chapter 5

"What are you doing?" Millie asked.

Nic opened the oven door and gingerly removed a loaf of bread. "I found your bread recipe and baggie on the counter and decided to surprise you."

"You baked the bread on the counter?"

"I was so wound up; I figured I wouldn't be able to sleep right away, so I thought I would help in the kitchen."

Millie burst out laughing. She doubled over, tears streaming down her cheeks. "Oh, Nic. I love you."

"I love you, too." There was a puzzled expression on his face as he watched Millie. "What's so funny about me baking in the kitchen?"

"It's the bread," Millie gasped. "It's friendship bread. You're supposed to spend ten days nurturing it before adding several more ingredients, and THEN you bake it in the oven."

"Do you mean I wasted my time and it won't taste good?" Nic looked miffed.

"I have no idea. You must've found the second set of instructions and missed the first where you babysit the mixture for ten days." Millie pressed a light finger on the top of the bread. "It seems to have baked. Honestly, it should be okay. The longer version of the recipe is more like wash, rinse and repeat."

"I hope so. I was looking forward to sampling it."

Millie grabbed the recipe off the counter. "I planned to add pudding, nuts and chocolate chips before baking it."

"I couldn't find any pudding, but we did have cinnamon, semi-sweet chocolate chips and chopped walnuts, so I added those."

Scout pranced into the kitchen, and Millie picked him up. "There's my sidekick."

The small pup licked Millie's chin, and she set him on the floor. "The bread looks delicious. I can't wait to try it, but it will have to wait until later. I'm on my way to co-host a foxtrot class."

Millie grabbed Scout's new harness and slipped it on. "You should try to get some rest."

"I'm heading upstairs shortly." Nic kissed his wife and pulled back. "Are you sure you're not upset about the bread?"

"Not in the least." Millie grinned as she placed a light hand on his cheek. "I know you were trying to surprise me by helping me out, which means it's my turn to return the favor."

Nic leaned in, his lids lowering. "What did you have in mind?"

"You'll have to wait and see," Millie flirted. She gave him a lingering kiss and reluctantly pulled away. "I better go before I change my mind, and Andy has to hunt me down."

*****

Alison, Millie's co-host, was already on stage, talking to a group of passengers when she and Scout arrived.

"What a cute pup." One of the passengers coaxed Scout to the edge of the stage. "What's your name?"

"Scout and he's spoiled rotten." The Yorkie made his rounds, lapping up the extra attention until the class began where even Millie learned a new step. After the class ended, they headed upstairs to begin a "Behind the Scenes" tour.

The morning passed quickly, and they stopped by the buffet to grab a quick bite to eat before heading to the Marseille Lounge for their art class.

Finally, there was a break in her schedule, and Millie decided to swing by the galley to tell Annette about Nic's surprise, how he'd baked the bread.

She found her friend on the telephone, a frantic look on her face. Millie had started to back out of the galley when Annette noticed her and motioned for her to stay.

"I see. Please...please call me if you hear anything." She hung up the phone. "Amit is missing. He never showed up for work this morning. I can't reach him on the phone or by radio. I sent someone to check his cabin. He's not answering his door."

"Oh no." Millie's eyes grew wide. "I have some free time between now and my next event. Would you like me to help you try to find him?"

"Could you? I'm really worried." Annette untied her apron and pulled it off. "We can split up and cover more ground."

"I agree. Maybe we can rustle up some extra help." Millie removed her radio and called Danielle. "What are you doing?"

"Hosting another singles mingle. What's up?"

"Amit is missing."

"Missing?"

"He never showed up for his shift this morning and isn't answering his door. I can't go into detail right now, but Annette and I are both concerned. We're getting ready to search the ship, and I was hoping you might have time to help us."

"Sure. The meet is wrapping up. Where do you want me to start?"

Millie decided she and Annette would search the lower crew decks while Danielle searched the upper passenger decks.

"I'll head up there now."

Millie replaced her radio and followed her friend out of the galley. "Call me if you hear anything."

Annette promised she would before making her way to the stairwell. Millie stopped to drop Scout off at home and then headed to deck zero and the maintenance area.

Her plan was to track down Sharky first. She stepped into the corridor and heard the maintenance supervisor before she saw him.

"And we gotta keep the halls clear. This ship is loaded to the gills. We still have eleven days before offloading the recycle stuff."

Millie rounded the corner and found him in the center of the hall standing on the seat of his scooter. Several maintenance workers stood nearby listening to him talk.

"We got a long trip ahead of us and need to make the most of every square inch of space. I don't wanna see any more stacked empty boxes. You gotta break each and every one down. No ifs, ands, or buts. " Sharky waved his unlit cigar in the air before plopping down on the seat.

The crewmembers jumped out of the way as he revved up the engine.

The scooter made a loud *bang*. A projectile shot out of the tailpipe and smashed into the wall.

Sharky scrambled off the scooter. His work boot tangled with the saddlebag strap and he tumbled to the ground. His cigar went airborne before hitting the concrete floor and bouncing off a piece of trim.

One of the maintenance workers hurried to help while several others chuckled at the sight of their boss sprawled out on the floor.

Enraged, Sharky pushed the man away and jumped to his feet. He stomped over to the cigar and snatched it up. "The next bozo I catch pranking my scooter is gonna get sewer sanitation for the next *month*." Sharky clenched his fists. "I'm sick and tired of your shenanigans."

One of the crewmembers snorted and then attempted to cover it with a cough.

"It ain't funny, and I ain't laughing." Sharky peeled the projectile - a bruised banana - from the wall and waved it in the air. "This means war!" he roared.

There was another chuckle from the crowd. Sharky's face turned bright red, and his expression became thunderous.

Millie took a step back, praying the man wasn't in the vicinity of some sort of weapon.

"You." Sharky took a measured step toward the crewmember who dared to laugh. "Think that's funny, Davis? You won't be laughing for the next two weeks while you have sewer sanitation duty."

"I..." The man's jaw dropped as he stumbled backward. "Jerk."

"Make it a month!" Sharky barked.

Davis pushed his way through the crowd and stomped off.

"Anyone else want to join Davis in cleaning out the sewer system?"

An uncomfortable silence followed.

"Get out of here."

The men hurried away, anxious to escape Sharky's wrath until only Millie and Sharky remained.

"Hey, Millie."

"Hey, Sharky. Seems like your men were having a little fun at your scooter's expense." Millie motioned to the mangled piece of fruit.

"They're a bunch of clowns." Sharky tossed the fruit in the recycle bin. "They get a little stir crazy and start pulling pranks. Most of it's innocent stuff, but they know better than to mess with The Sharkmeister's ride."

He changed the subject. "So what brings you to my neck of the woods?"

"I was wondering if Amit Uddin, the employee who works in Annette's kitchen, was hanging around down here."

"Amit." Sharky tapped his chin thoughtfully. "Is he the skinny little guy with the black hair who's always hanging around my babe?"

Millie smiled. "Yeah. That's him. He's MIA. Annette hasn't seen him since yesterday. He's not in his cabin and not in the common areas. I thought

74

you might have crossed paths since you're all over this part of the ship."

"Nope." Sharky shook his head. "I'll let you know if I run into him."

"Thanks." Millie turned to go.

"Hey."

She turned back. "Yeah?"

"Heard about the entertainer chick who went over the side of the ship last night." Sharky made a diving motion with his hands. "What a rough way to go."

"Yes, it is. Nic said they recovered her body, which was nothing short of a miracle."

"The guys manning the rescue boats stopped by here after the body was recovered."

"I haven't heard whether she jumped or if someone pushed her," Millie said.

"My guess is she had a little help." Sharky climbed onto his scooter.

"Why do you say that?"

"Because one of the guys - Mateo - said she had a scratch, some sort of injury on her neck."

Millie's heart skipped a beat. "Maybe she cut herself."

"Maybe. To me, it seems suspicious, but what do I know?" Sharky started his scooter. "I wasn't supposed to be privy to that information, so you never heard it from me."

"My lips are sealed." Millie made a zipping motion across her lips. "Thanks for the info."

"You're welcome." Sharky reached for the handle. "What's Annette up to these days?"

"She's working, and she's worried sick over Amit."

"He'll turn up," Sharky waved dismissively. "It's not like you can go missing on a cruise ship...unless you go overboard." He started to pull away and then stopped. "When you see Annette, tell her Sharky said 'hi.'"

"I will." Millie waited for Sharky and his scooter to roar off. He careened around the corner, tires squealing, before disappearing from sight.

Despite Sharky's comment that he hadn't seen Amit, she searched deck zero, bow to stern before climbing the stairs to deck one and the crew quarters. Along the way, she stopped several of the crewmembers to ask if anyone had seen him, but no one had.

The longer Millie searched, the more concerned she became that something terrible had happened to her friend...and it was her fault. She silently prayed for Amit, that they would find him.

Millie finished her search and stepped outside to radio Danielle. "Any luck?"

"Not yet. I'm almost done. I'm gonna do a quick check of the crew's outdoor entertaining area."

"Annette and I will meet you there." Millie caught up with her friend on an upper deck, and then they met Danielle near the entrance to the crewmember's hot tub area, which was also the location of the ship's helipad.

The women split up, with Millie and Annette making their way to the back while Danielle strode to the covered patio area next to the hot tub.

Millie checked the restroom first. It was empty. Next up was the shuffleboard court. A stiff wind blew off the front of the ship, and a mist of saltwater pelted the side of her face.

She stumbled back, steering clear of the spray zone before walking past another secluded area and a small cluster of tables and chairs.

The deck was a popular hangout for the younger crewmembers. It was far away from the activities of the passengers, and few knew it even existed, which was fine with the crew. It gave them a much-needed break from their hectic, non-stop workdays.

She began to backtrack when she heard Danielle's frantic voice call out from the other side of the deck. "Millie! Annette! Come quick!"

Chapter 6

The women raced to the other side of the hot tub where they found Danielle leaning over Amit who was sprawled out on the deck. "Amit. Can you hear me?"

Annette fell to her knees and reached for his hand. "Amit."

Amit let out a low moan, and his eyelids fluttered.

"We need help." Millie reached for her radio, and he started to stir.

"Miss Annette?" Amit mumbled. "What are you doing?"

"Looking for you. What are you doing out here?"

A dazed Amit blinked rapidly. "Where am I?"

"You're outdoors by the crewmembers' hot tubs."

He pressed a hand to the side of his head. "I...I remember coming out here last night because I couldn't sleep. I sat down, and that is the last thing I remember."

Annette leaned in. "Did you take something, maybe too many sleeping pills?"

"I took a sleeping pill, but only one. What time is it?"

"It's past noon." Danielle grasped his arm as he struggled to his feet.

"Noon? I'm sorry, Miss Annette."

"It's okay, Amit. I'm just glad we found you."

Millie and Annette stepped in on each side of Amit and helped him to the door while Danielle ran ahead to hold it open.

"You should stop by Doctor Gundervan's office to get checked out. You may have had an adverse reaction to the sleeping pill. What was it?" Millie asked.

"I don't know. I got it from one of my friends. He said it was good for sleeping."

"You don't know what you took?" Annette gasped. "Do you have any idea how dangerous that is?"

"I won't be doing it again. I'm feeling much better. I think it knocked me out very good." He began to sway.

"A trip to the medical center is in order," Annette said firmly.

Amit took a tentative step and tripped on the edge of the carpet.

Millie lunged forward to steady him. "It's settled. We're definitely going to visit Doctor Gundervan. We'll take the elevator." She forced her claustrophobia from her mind and jabbed the elevator's down button. Thankfully, it was empty.

Annette guided Amit inside while Millie pressed the button for deck two.

"You guys have this under control," Danielle said. "I need to head to my next event. Call me with an update."

"We will," Millie promised.

They reached deck two and exited the elevator. It was a slow trek to the other end of the ship and the medical center.

Millie jogged ahead and held the door while Annette and Amit cautiously made their way inside.

Siren of the Seas' new nurse, Gavin Framm, hurried from the back to offer a hand. "What happened?"

"Amit took a sleeping aid last night. We found him groggy and semi-conscious on one of the upper decks. We were hoping Doctor Gundervan could take a quick look at him," Annette explained.

"Of course. The doctor is in the back." Gavin guided Amit to the examining room while Annette and Millie stayed behind.

Doctor Gundervan emerged a short time later. "Amit is going to be okay. He's still suffering from the effects of the sleep aid."

"Thank God," Annette said.

"Do you know what he took?" Millie asked. "He was totally whacked out."

"I don't." The doctor glanced over his shoulder and lowered his voice. "I suspect it was a street drug. He's lucky it only conked him out. We don't need another body in the holding area."

"Absolutely not," Millie agreed. "Nic told me this morning the searchers found Wendy Rainwell's body, which is nothing short of a miracle."

"Her arm was tangled around a life preserver someone had tossed over the side," Gundervan said. "An autopsy will determine the actual cause of death."

"And perhaps even her wound?" Millie asked.

"Nic told you the woman showed signs of injury?" Gundervan frowned.

"No. I...uh...found out from another source. So she somehow managed to grab onto a life preserver."

"Both crewmembers and passengers began tossing them over the side of the ship. My guess is she must have managed to grab one. While she waited to be rescued, she succumbed to her injuries. The reflective life preserver helped searchers find her," Gundervan said. "An autopsy will be performed after Ms. Rainwell's body is taken off the ship in Bermuda and flown back to the States."

Doctor Gundervan motioned to Annette. "Did you get the message I left you yesterday?"

"I did," Annette lowered her gaze. "I've been meaning to get down here, but it's been so busy, I forgot."

The doctor turned to Millie. "Do you mind if I have a word alone with Annette?"

"Of course not." Millie gave her friend a quick smile and stepped into the hall. She watched as Doctor Gundervan reached into the filing cabinet behind him. He pulled out a file folder, flipped it open and then handed something to Annette.

Millie couldn't hear what the doctor was saying, but Annette's expression grew solemn. She nodded and then carefully folded the piece of paper before shoving it into her pocket.

The doctor's expression matched Annette's as he placed a light hand on her shoulder and said something else.

The exchange ended when a pale Amit and Nurse Framm emerged from the back. Millie returned to the waiting room.

"Mr. Uddin claims he's feeling much better and is ready to leave."

"Stubborn as a mule," Annette said. "I'm sure you'll agree Amit isn't ready to return to work."

"No. He needs to rest." Gundervan addressed his patient with a solemn tone. "Do not, under any circumstances, take medication or sleep aids from friends."

"Yes, sir. I will be more cautious in the future." Amit thanked the doctor for examining him, and the trio exited the medical center.

When they reached Amit's cabin, he slipped his keycard in the slot and pushed the door open. "Thank you for finding me."

"You're welcome," Millie said. "You scared us half to death."

"Mostly me." Annette's radio went off. It was one of the kitchen crewmembers sounding frantic. "We have a small emergency in the kitchen."

"I'm on my way." Annette cast her friends a hesitant glance.

"I'll make sure he gets settled in," Millie promised. "Besides, I want to chat with him for a minute while I'm here."

"Thanks, Millie." Annette wagged her finger at Amit. "Stay put. I'll be back to check on you later."

Annette hurried off while Amit motioned for Millie to join him in his cabin before closing the door behind them. "You are wondering about Wendy Rainwell. Mr. Patterson called me to his office to ask me about her."

"I'm sorry, Amit. I saw you talking to Wendy last night. I only heard a couple of words of your conversation. She was looking for a man who worked in the kitchen, to tell him she was pregnant."

"And you thought it was me."

"Yes," Millie whispered. "I heard the word baby and child support and assumed..." Her voice trailed off.

"I told Mr. Patterson that I knew Wendy. She was a regular at Azure. I haven't been hanging around there since Carlah and I started dating. When

Wendy got on board, she tracked me down and asked me to help her find the baby's father."

"Did she give you a name?" Millie asked.

"She said his name was Jerry Dean. There is no one who works in Miss Annette's kitchen by that name."

"So the baby's father lied to her." Millie began to pace. "Which means he could have lied about working in the kitchen or even on board our ship. Did Wendy tell you what he looked like?"

"Yes." Amit nodded. "He is my height, with dark hair and brown eyes. He works on this ship. Wendy told me she walked him to the ship one night and watched him pass through the security gate after showing the guard his card."

"And yet she never saw his card to verify his name?"

Amit shrugged. "I don't know. All I know is Wendy tracked me down last night to ask if Jerry

Dean worked with me. I told her I didn't know anyone by that name. She was very distraught."

"I can imagine," Millie murmured. "She must've realized the man lied to her. Did she mention him having any unique features, moles or perhaps a birthmark?"

"No. Nothing." Amit's hand trembled as he touched the front of his forehead.

"You should get some rest," Millie said worriedly.

"Yes. I think I need to lie down." Amit kicked off his shoes and crawled onto his bunk.

Millie waited for her friend to settle in before stepping out of his cabin. If what Amit said was true, and she had no reason not to believe him, the father of Wendy's baby was lying about his identity.

Wendy claimed he passed through the checkpoint leading to their ship, which meant he worked on Siren of the Seas. Had she tracked down the baby's father, they argued, he attacked her and then tossed her over the side of the ship?

Millie made her way to the galley and found Annette standing at the counter studying a small slip of paper. She quickly shoved it in her pocket when she spotted Millie. "How's Amit?"

"Hopefully, he's napping by now."

"He just took ten years off my life."

"Mine, too." Millie hesitated for a second. "Is everything okay?"

"Other than Amit going missing and a woman going overboard?"

"No," Millie said softly. "I mean with Doctor Gundervan in his office."

"Oh that." Annette waved dismissively. "I have a referral appointment to see a specialist when we reach Southampton. Gundervan is making a big deal about it."

"But you're okay?" Millie asked.

"I'm healthy as a horse."

Annette's voice was firm, but Millie detected a hint of concern. "If you want someone to go with you, I'll be happy to tag along."

"Thanks."

Millie could see her friend didn't want to discuss whatever it was. She changed the subject and pointed to a cake dish. "Are you still tweaking your teatime recipes?"

"Always." Annette was tinkering with treats to "up her game" for the ship's formal afternoon tea. One of her most recent changes was adding a classic scone with jam and clotted cream. She set the knife on the counter. "I'm guessing you stayed behind to talk to Amit about Wendy."

"I did." Millie briefly explained her conversation with Amit, how he met Wendy at the club, and after she boarded the ship, she tracked him down to help her find the baby's father. "The man lied about his identity. There's a chance he works in your kitchen, or in one of the kitchens. Wendy's description could be any one of the hundreds of crewmembers - dark hair, around Amit's height with brown eyes."

She rattled off the name Wendy had given Amit. "Does the name ring a bell?"

"Nope." Annette shook her head. "Even if Jerry Dean doesn't work directly for me, I know the names of all of the daytime kitchen staff."

An employee approached to ask Annette a question, and Millie headed out. Her next stop was Andy's office to go over his special "surprise." Danielle, Isla and Andy were already there.

Andy waved her in. "Good...good. Thanks for being on time, Millie." He rubbed his hands together. "As you all know, I've been working on a very special surprise for the entertainment staff."

Andy reached into the cardboard box in front of him and pulled out a smaller box. "This right here is going to change the future of the cruise ship entertainment industry."

Chapter 7

Millie squinted her eyes. "What is it?"

"It's a watch app." Andy handed Danielle, Isla and Millie each a box. "I've programmed all three of these with tomorrow's work schedule. I figured since we have a port day in Bermuda, we'll have time to practice using it."

Millie flipped the top on the box. Nestled inside was a watch, the face of it a black square. She pulled it out and unclasped the cheap blue band.

"It's ugly." Danielle dangled the strap of her bright red watch. "How come Millie gets the blue one?"

"At least you don't have this one," Isla joked as she displayed her lime green watch.

"I gave each of you a different color for tracking purposes. Try them on." Andy lifted his arm to display a watch identical to theirs except his boasted a black wristband and a larger face. "Mine has the motherboard so I can transmit schedule updates to key staff...namely, you three, at least to start with."

He eagerly waited for the women to strap the watches to their wrists.

"How do we..." Millie's screen suddenly lit up. "It just came on."

"I'm controlling it." The expression on Andy's face reminded Millie of a mad scientist as he gleefully began tapping the top of his mini screen.

"Welcome to SOSES," Danielle read the words on the screen. "Siren of the Seas Entertainment Software. It's still loading."

The introduction screen disappeared, and another screen replaced it. The words were tiny, and Millie squinted her eyes. "The print is small."

"Ah, ha." Andy pointed his finger in the air. "I knew some of you...Millie, in particular, might have trouble seeing the screen." Continuing in mad scientist mode, he grabbed a stylus and began tapping the screen.

"Ack." Millie's watch vibrated, and she jumped.

"Sorry," Andy snickered. "Not only does the watch have audio and visual, but it also has a vibration function. All of the watches are in audio and visual mode. Tap the top."

Isla tapped the top. *Schedule for Monday, April 16th. Isla Petersen. Eight a.m. Daily Brain Teasers, Library deck four. Nine a.m. VIP Pampering Party, Spa deck twelve. Ten a.m. Early Risers Trivia.*

The monotone voice continued, rattling off the day's schedule.

"Is there a way to shut it off?" Isla asked.

"Tap the screen," Andy said. "Tap the screen once for the visual schedule, tap it twice for audio and visual and tap it a third time to shut it off. There's another special surprise but I don't want to tell you about it yet."

"I can hardly wait," Danielle muttered.

"So?" Andy beamed excitedly. "What do you think?"

"It's...interesting," Millie attempted to muster some enthusiasm.

"It's an invasion," Danielle joked. "How is this going to help us?"

"I can add to or change the schedule on the fly without having to track you down on the radio, especially if you're in the middle of an event. The watch will notify each of you of the change."

Andy finished pointing out a few of the watches' other features and then stood. "Tomorrow is our trial run. I need each of you to wear the scheduler the entire day, and then we'll meet tomorrow evening. Be prepared to give me your feedback."

"Oh, boy," Isla slid her chair back. "This should be exciting."

Millie and Danielle followed her out of Andy's office, and Millie waited until they were out of earshot to speak. "What do you think?"

"I'm on the fence with this one," Isla said.

"I guess I am, too," Danielle said. "It strikes me as a little overkill. After all, why fix something that isn't broken?"

Andy's door flew open. "I was so excited, I almost forgot. Blackjack Blaze needs an assistant for his show. It's only until the ship reaches Southampton. I was thinking either you, Danielle, or Isla would be the perfect candidate."

Danielle and Isla exchanged a nervous glance.

"Assistant?" Isla wrinkled her nose.

"We're going to hold a mini-audition at six, which coincides with the main seating dining," Andy said. "Meet me in the Kickstart Comedy Den on deck six at six."

"Deck six at six," Isla repeated.

"What if I refuse?" Danielle asked.

"You can't. This is a mandatory tryout." Andy patted Danielle's arm. "Don't worry. You might actually enjoy it. Blackjack promised me he wouldn't try to cut you in half."

"That's comforting," Danielle groaned. "Why can't Millie fill in?"

"Because I have other plans for her. Millie's schedule is booked for this entire trip. I'll see both of you in a couple of hours." Andy returned to his office and closed the door behind him.

"I guess we don't have to leave these on until tomorrow." Millie unfastened the watch, and it vibrated again. It slipped out of her hand and fell to the floor. "The vibration is going to drive me crazy."

"No kidding," Danielle said. "Ten bucks says Andy's handy dandy control center alerts him when we take them off."

"Like a criminal's ankle monitor, except for the wrist," Millie joked.

"I wouldn't be surprised," Isla chuckled. "I'll see you later for our auditions."

Danielle grimaced. "Yeah. I can hardly wait."

Millie's dinner break was up next. She grabbed a healthy version of a chicken Caesar wrap and headed outdoors. The skies had turned dark, and a stiff breeze whipped around the corner of the bar area. Off in the distance, she could see storm clouds gathering.

Millie paid little attention to the weather forecast unless she planned to get off the ship on a port day. The only other time she kept an eye on the weather was during hurricane season, and the ship was heading toward a storm.

It started to drizzle, so she gobbled her food and dashed inside before deciding to head up to the Sky Chapel to say hello to Pastor Pete Evans.

The chapel was dark, and the lights were off. Millie wandered down the center aisle and eased onto a front pew. She gazed at the cross before clasping her hands and bowing her head.

She thanked God for all of her blessings. She prayed for her children, her grandchildren, for Nic and for her friends. Millie prayed for smooth sailing and that the Lord would help ease her homesickness as she poured out her heart over her concerns. Last, but not least, she prayed for Wendy Rainwell and her family.

Creak. Millie lifted her head as Pastor Evans emerged from a side entrance. His eyes scanned the dark chapel until he spied Millie.

He made his way over. "Hello, Millie."

"Hello, Pastor Evans. I had a few minutes and decided it was the perfect time to catch my breath and pray."

"I'm sorry. I didn't mean to interrupt."

"You're not. I've finished." Millie slid to the side to make room. "Are you enjoying our trip so far?"

"I am." The pastor joined her. "As you know, I've tossed around the idea of retiring and buying a log cabin in Tennessee to be near my children and grandchildren."

"Have you decided?"

"Not yet. I've been praying about it. It's a big decision. I figured a cruise around the isles would help clear my head." Pastor Evans leaned back and eyed Millie. "How are you?"

"I'm still anxious over the thought of being so far from home, but also looking forward to the adventures."

"You'll have a fine time, Millie." The pastor changed the subject. "I heard about the poor woman, Wendy Rainwell, who went over the side of the ship last night."

"Yes. It's a horrible tragedy."

"Her boss, Blackjack Blaze, stopped by here earlier. He's taking Ms. Rainwell's death hard."

"I'm sure he is."

Pastor Evans leaned forward, placing his elbows on his knees. "We must be prepared to meet our maker at any time."

The watch scheduler Millie had shoved in her jacket pocket vibrated, and she jumped.

"Are you okay?"

"Andy Walker." Millie grabbed the annoying object. "Andy is testing a new entertainment scheduler. It keeps vibrating and scaring me half to death."

The pastor chuckled. "Better you than me."

Millie tapped the screen. *Trivia at casino bar. Entertainment audition. Kickstart Comedy Den at six*, the monotone voice reminded her.

"I better get going. Good luck on your decision. I'll add you to my prayer list."

"I can use all the help I can get." Pastor Evans thanked Millie for the prayers, and then she made her way out of the chapel.

The trivia hour flew by. Up next was Isla and Danielle's auditions. Isla, Andy and Blackjack were already inside the comedy den. Danielle was notably missing.

"Where's Danielle?" Millie asked.

"I don't know," Andy said. "I sent her a reminder."

"You mean you zapped her, too?" Millie joked.

"He zapped us all," Isla said. "Please...I'm begging you to turn that thing off."

Andy looked crestfallen. "You don't like the zap app?"

"No," Millie shook her head. "It's scaring me half to death."

"Fine. I'll try to figure out a way to disable it."

The door flew open, and Danielle stormed inside. "Andy Walker, if this thing zaps me one more time, I'm going to toss it over the side of the ship."

Millie chuckled. "Three for three. You better figure out a way to turn it off, or you'll have a mini-mutiny on your hands."

"I will." Andy rubbed his hands together. "It's time to get this audition underway." He motioned to Blackjack. "We've discovered a small issue concerning the entertainment show. I'm going to let Blackjack explain our dilemma."

Chapter 8

Blackjack cleared his throat. "First, let me tell you about my show, Sea-Fi. It's part optical illusion, part comedy, and all magic...with a flair for the extraordinaire." He rolled his right wrist, and a bouquet of flowers materialized.

He handed it to Danielle. "For you, my lovely lady." He repeated the trick, and with a small bow handed the second bouquet to Isla. "Our guests expect, and should receive, an award-winning, mind-blowing show."

Danielle cut to the chase. "What is the 'small dilemma' Andy mentioned?"

"Attire. My assistant is required to wear an evening gown for each of the shows," Blackjack said bluntly. "My ensemble includes a top hat, coat and tails, and my lovely assistant wears an elegant evening gown."

"We have plenty to choose from," Andy chimed in.

"Count me out," Danielle stubbornly shook her head. "I've only worn one dress in the last decade, and it was for Millie and the captain's wedding. Never again, not even for my funeral."

"Isla..." Andy slowly turned to the woman standing next to Danielle.

"I'm with Danielle. Casual khakis are more my style."

"Blackjack needs an assistant," Andy argued. "We're running out of time."

"What about one of the female entertainers - Alison or Tara?" Danielle asked.

"They won't work. Both women are part of the pre-show."

"Draw straws," Millie suggested. "It's the only fair way."

"Well?" Danielle eyed Isla.

"Sure. Straws it is."

Millie darted out of the club and to the nearest bar. She grabbed four straws and asked the bartender to snip the ends in various lengths before joining Andy and the others.

Millie grasped the straws tightly. "By seniority, Danielle draws first."

Danielle plucked out a straw. Isla followed suit.

"Aha." Isla triumphantly waved the longer of the two straws. "That was a close one."

"Crud." Danielle frowned at her shorter straw. "This was rigged from the get-go."

"It was not," Millie laughed. "You lost fair and square. Do you want me to help you pick out the evening gowns?"

Danielle whacked her friend in the arm. "It's not funny."

"Don't be such a spoilsport." Andy whisked Danielle to the front of the stage where Blackjack stood waiting.

While the others discussed the specifics, Isla pulled Millie off to the side. "I saw the security guys searching Wendy Rainwell's cabin earlier today. Word on the street is she either jumped or was pushed overboard."

"I heard the same," Millie whispered back.

"What about him?" Isla motioned to Blackjack. "Is he a suspect? Maybe we should keep an eye on Danielle."

"Not a bad idea. I'm sure he's on Patterson's radar."

Andy joined them, abruptly ending their conversation. They sat in the front row, watching a reluctant Danielle and an animated Blackjack run through a rough rehearsal. After finishing, Millie offered to help Danielle sort through the stage costumes.

"If we have to," Danielle said glumly.

"I'll go with you." Isla consulted Andy's special watch. "I have time before my 'Evening Under the Stars' golf lesson on the sky deck starts."

Millie checked her schedule. "I'm free until seven-ish when we're hosting a past guest party in the dance club."

"Great," Andy patted Millie on the back. "I'm sure the three of you can come up with some smashing outfits for Danielle."

"I owe you one, Andy Walker." Danielle lifted her arm and tapped the top of the activity watch. "And if this thing goes off while I'm on stage, I'm going to remove one of those ridiculous stiletto heels Blackjack is insisting I wear and pop you in the back of the head."

Andy's eyes widened. "There's no need to threaten me with violence, Danielle. I promised I would try to adjust the settings, and I will."

The look of revenge lingered in Danielle's eyes, and Millie quickly led her out of the comedy club.

Isla hurried to catch up. "I'm sorry you got the short end of the straw," she apologized. "At least it's only for a couple of weeks."

"Isla is right. Look on the bright side. It's only temporary."

"Easy for you two to say," Danielle sighed. "There's something about that guy. He makes my skin crawl, and he kept giving me an evil leer."

Isla rubbed the sides of her arms. "You got that vibe, too? I thought I was imagining it."

The women reached the theater where Felix, one of the dancers, was teaching a disco class. He winked at Millie, and she gave him a small wave.

The backstage dressing area was empty. Millie unlocked the costume closet next to the dressing room and began rummaging around inside. "Let's see what we've got." She eyed Danielle critically. "You're thin but kinda tall."

"How about this one?" Isla removed a vintage lacy red Victorian gown with a floral-patterned jacket. A thick ruffle circled the neckline and cascaded to the floor.

Danielle made a gagging sound. "This would be perfect for a masquerade party, but I would never make it there alive because the ruffled neckline would choke me first."

"Here's one." Millie held up a jet black, full-length ballroom gown. The top of the bodice was laced with an intricate design of crystals and rhinestones. "This one screams classy."

"Classy?" Danielle gave it a thumbs down. "More like I'm on my way to a fancy funeral."

There were quick steps behind them, and Felix appeared. "I thought I heard voices back here. What are you doing?"

"We're trying to find some evening gowns for Danielle. So far, she doesn't like any of our picks," Millie explained.

Felix sashayed across the room and pulled Danielle from her chair. "I would love to help." He eyed Danielle's frame. "You have the shape of a hot tamale, dear. You could wear a gunny sack and look sex-y."

"I don't want to look sexy," Danielle groaned. "Do you think you could find me something more along the lines of invisible?"

Felix ignored the comment and tapped the tip of his chin. "We want something that screams 'look at me.'" He pulled a silver sleeveless one-shoulder sweep from the rack and held it to her.

Danielle shook her head. "Nope. Way too much cleavage and leg showing."

"What about this one? The coloring is perfect for your long, luscious locks." He removed a coral colored spandex dress. Amethyst appliques edged the bodice while a band of turquoise rhinestone accents circled the waistline.

"Whoa." Danielle clamped her hand over her eyes. "Those colors...they're burning my retina."

Felix placed his hand on his hip. "Aren't we the diva? Danielle, the Diva."

"I'm not a diva. I just don't like dresses."

"Wait." Felix snapped his fingers. "I think I found it...the perfect dress." He placed the rhinestone-studded dress back in the closet before carefully removing a stunning sapphire maxi dress. The front was a deep V-neck and sported pale blue crystals that twinkled beneath the stage lights.

"This might work." Millie nodded approvingly. "The color is stunning."

Felix turned it over. Spaghetti straps crisscrossed in the back, attaching to a snug waistline that billowed into a flowing maxi skirt.

"The dress is beautiful," Isla ran a light hand over the fabric. "Is this new?"

"It is. We just got it in, along with a few other pieces for the upcoming season." He held it to Danielle. "Well?"

She started to shake her head.

"Danielle," Millie warned.

"What? I'm being honest. It's pretty if you like that sort of thing."

"Try it on." Millie took the dress from Felix and passed it to Danielle.

"Do I have to?"

"Yes. Now."

"Fine." Danielle stomped off, and Millie turned to Felix. "Thank you for rescuing us. You have an eye for design. It's a beautiful dress."

"You're welcome," Felix grinned. "Miss Danielle, she is going to join the other performers on stage?"

"Sort of. I'm sure you heard about the death of the new entertainer, Wendy Rainwell."

Felix's expression clouded. "Yes. What a terrible tragedy."

Danielle returned to the stage, carefully lifting the bottom of the gown to keep it from dragging, a frown firmly in place.

"Ah. Yes." Felix made a twirling motion with his finger. "Turn around so we can see the back."

She slowly turned, and Millie gasped. "It's a beautiful dress, Danielle. You should see it."

"No thanks. I'll take your word for it."

Millie gathered Danielle's long locks and held them up. "If we fix her hair in a smooth upsweep, I do believe we have runway model material on our hands."

"You're drop-dead gorgeous," Isla chimed in. "This dress was made for you."

"Yeah, well, they should've made it for someone else. It's making me itch." Danielle gathered the hem again and tromped off stage.

"She's a natural beauty," Felix turned to Millie. "You mentioned the dead woman, Wendy. Is Danielle taking her place?"

"Yes. She'll be assisting Blackjack Blaze for the duration of the cruise."

"I was thinking about him earlier...this Blackjack Blaze," Felix said. "It just dawned on me. I think I've heard his name before."

Chapter 9

"You know him?" Millie asked.

"I know of him," Felix replied. "Have you heard of Cruise Careers?"

"I have," Isla answered. "It's an online website for cruise ship jobs."

"Blackjack Blaze posted an assistant's position not long ago. I remember his name. I even remember the name of his show - sea something."

"Sea-Fi instead of Sci-Fi," Millie said.

"Yes. That's it. Sea-Fi."

"So Blackjack posted a help-wanted ad on the site for an assistant," Millie repeated.

"I'm almost certain of it. In fact, the posting may still be up."

"Which means it's possible Wendy was getting ready to quit or Blackjack planned to fire her." Millie mulled over the information. Perhaps she told Blackjack she was thinking about quitting. Maybe Wendy decided with a baby on the way, she no longer wanted to work on board cruise ships.

Danielle returned with the dress in hand. "I won't need this until tomorrow night."

"I separated a few more I'm certain will work for some of the other shows." Felix placed the gown inside the cabinet and locked it. "I'll be here to root you on, Danielle. Millie is right. You should get your hair done. You'll look absolutely fab."

"I was aiming for invisible," Danielle joked.

"Honey, the last thing you'll be in that dress is invisible."

"That's what I'm afraid of." Danielle thanked Felix for his input, and the women stepped out of the dressing room.

It was time for Millie to head to the dance club for the past guest party. She arrived at the same time the guests began trickling in, and stood near the door collecting their admission tickets as she greeted them.

The tickets were something Andy recently implemented, after discovering some clever passengers were sneaking in uninvited. He let one or two slip through, but the crowds continued to grow, forcing the cruise line to begin collecting tickets at the door.

Andy joined the party alongside Nic, who attempted to slip past the crowd until a group of diamond guests cornered him.

He chatted with them for several moments before catching his wife's eye and making his way across the room. "Where have you been all day?"

"I didn't want to bother you while you were sleeping. How was the friendship bread?"

"Delicious. I saved you a small piece," he teased.

Andy stepped onto the stage to begin his presentation.

"That's my cue." Nic strode down the aisle as Andy introduced him.

Millie stood in the back and listened to the spiel, how honored and humbled Majestic Cruise Lines was to have the past guests once again choose them for their cruise vacation.

Following Nic's speech was a short video presentation, showing each of the cruise line's ships from past to present.

The video ended, and Nic passed out several awards...one to a woman who started cruising in the mid-70s and had hit a whopping 1,688 days at sea. It took several moments for the woman to reach the stage and accept her engraved plaque.

Nic handed her the mic, urging her to say a few words.

"Thank you, Captain Armati. I'm often asked why I love to cruise, and my favorite answer is because of all of the hot captains I've met over the years, including Captain Armati."

"Thank you," Nic smiled politely.

"Can I kiss you?" the woman brazenly asked.

"Kiss me?"

"You know...kiss the captain."

Millie burst out laughing at the flustered expression on her husband's face. He managed to recover with a snappy comeback. He leaned forward and pretended to whisper in her ear. "But my wife is in the back watching."

The woman gazed into the audience, and Millie waved before giving her the okay signal.

The woman smiled widely. "Your wife said it's okay."

The audience chuckled.

Nic bent down and lightly kissed the woman's cheek. "And here's to many more cruises, Bethany."

Andy swapped places with Nic, who helped the woman off the stage. He introduced the hotel director, the chief engineer, one of the executive chefs and the head of housekeeping. He finished the introductions and then a string quartet began to play while couples stepped on stage.

Millie circled the room, stopping to chat with several of the passengers. She found Nic near the back, attempting to make an escape.

"It seems as if you have a huge fan," she teased. "Should I be jealous?"

"Absolutely," Nic said. "When are you coming home?"

Millie consulted her handy-dandy Andy watch. "I'm doing late night karaoke at ten-thirty, so I should be in around midnight."

"You bought a new watch?"

"No. This is Andy's new experiment. It's a scheduling watch. He's asked Danielle, Isla and me to test it. So far, the jury is still out. If he can figure out how to get the darn thing to stop zapping us, we might be more inclined to like it."

"Zap?" Nic chuckled.

"It's not funny," Millie frowned. "Every time he makes a change to our work schedule, it vibrates."

"Poor Andy."

"Poor Andy? What about poor me?"

"I'm sure you'll sort it out. I hate to leave, but it's time for me to head back to work."

Millie reached out to stop him. "About that kiss...you owe me one."

"I do?" Nic's eyes met his wife's eyes. "Of course I do. You can collect later." He winked at her before sauntering off.

The party lasted for another half hour before the crowds cleared and the entertainment staff began setting up for the Heart and Home Show.

Millie made her rounds from the top of the ship to the bottom. When she reached deck seven, she decided to swing by Annette's kitchen to check on Amit. He was nowhere in sight.

Annette was there, standing in front of the stove. "Hey, Millie."

"I figured Amit would be here."

"He was. There's something up."

"Up as in the investigation up?"

"Brody was by here earlier looking for Amit. He said Patterson wanted to talk to him, so he accompanied him down to the security office. He hasn't come back yet."

"You don't think Patterson locked him in the holding cell, do you?" Millie shifted her feet. "He would have to have some sort of evidence against Amit to hold him."

"I don't know, but I'm growing more concerned by the minute. Before they left, I asked Brody why Patterson wanted to talk to Amit again. He was very evasive. I could tell by the way he was acting that he knows something."

"Where is Brody?"

"My guess is the casino area. At least that's where he was working earlier. I think he's avoiding me."

"I'll see if I can get Brody to spill the beans." Millie thanked her friend for the information and stepped into the corridor. The casino was mid-ship and on the same deck as the galley. She found Brody near the casino entrance and next to the bar area. "Hey, Brody."

"Hey, Millie. Haven't seen you around for a couple of days."

"Andy is keeping us hopping. Danielle was coerced into filling in for Wendy Rainwell as Blackjack Blaze's assistant."

"Danielle?" Brody lifted a brow.

"Not by choice since she's required to wear an evening gown for the shows."

"Now this I've gotta see," Brody grinned.

"She's not the least bit happy about it. You should see one of the dresses we picked out for her. It took my breath away." Brody and Danielle had stopped seeing each other some time back. Neither would go into detail about what exactly had happened and Millie, determined to mind her own business for once, vowed to keep her nose out of it.

"Annette thinks you uncovered something new in the Wendy Rainwell investigation which is why Patterson wanted to talk to Amit again."

"Right." Brody nodded.

"And..." Millie prompted.

"You know I can't talk, Millie. Patterson would have my hide."

"Can you at least give me a hint? Does it involve her boss, Blackjack Blaze?"

"Maybe."

"So it does involve Blackjack."

"Maybe, which means it could be either a yes or no answer," Brody said.

Millie decided to try a different angle. "Have you searched Wendy's cabin?"

Brody flinched, and Millie knew she was onto something.

"You found something in Wendy's cabin."

"Are you trying to get me fired?"

"No. I would never do that," Millie clasped her hands, her mind whirling. "I'm sure Patterson gathered Wendy's belongings and plans to return them to her family when we dock in Bermuda tomorrow."

"It stands to reason," Brody vaguely replied.

"Which means if you found some sort of evidence, you found it today."

Brody stared stone-faced, but his lower lip started to twitch.

"So if I happened to be in the vicinity of Wendy's cabin, and I happened to see the door ajar and stepped inside to make sure no one was in there, I *might* find something."

A flicker crossed Brody's face. He quickly recovered. "The cabin is empty. Patterson removed all of the items."

"You're no help." Millie stomped her foot in frustration.

"Good, then I've done my job," Brody said. "I care about what happens to Amit, too. He's a good guy."

"I know." Millie sighed heavily. "Thanks for the non-information." She told Brody good-bye and slowly strolled out of the bar area. There was something in his expression when she questioned him about Wendy's cabin, some flicker of something.

Was there a clue inside the woman's cabin? If so, did it implicate Amit? Otherwise, why would Patterson bring him in for questioning again?

Millie returned to the galley and found her friend in the same spot. She stood staring blankly into space as if she were a million miles away. "Annette?"

Annette's head snapped back. "Hey, Millie. Did you track down Brody?"

"I did and he was tight-lipped, so I kept guessing. I could tell from the expression on his face that Patterson may have found something in Wendy's cabin, some sort of clue."

"I'm sure the contents have been confiscated, and Patterson stashed them in a safe place."

"Yeah." Millie leaned her hip on the cabinet. "You're probably right, but I'm thinking there might still be something inside. It wouldn't hurt to run down there to have a quick look around."

"We should go together." Annette wiped her hands on the front of her apron. "Two sets of eyes are better than one."

"I'm hosting a couple more rounds of trivia, and then I have late night karaoke until around eleven-thirty. Is that too late to run by there?"

"No." Annette shook her head. "The timing will work. Most of the evening staff will have knocked off by then, and there shouldn't be too many crewmembers hanging around the crew corridor."

The women agreed to meet at eleven-forty, and Millie headed out to begin her last few events. She kept one eye on her watch as the time dragged. Finally, eleven-forty arrived.

As Annette predicted, the crew areas were empty. Millie turned onto the crew corridor where she found her friend waiting. "Right on time."

"This way." Millie and Annette fell into step, moving at a brisk pace until they reached crew cabin C110.

"This is it." Millie used her master keycard to open the cabin door. The women slipped inside, and she quietly closed the door behind them.

Annette ran the back of her elbow along the wall until she found the light switch. She reached into her pocket and pulled out two pairs of rubber gloves, handing a pair to Millie. "We don't want to contaminate the cabin if there's still potential evidence in here."

"You're right." Millie tugged the gloves on as she glanced around. "Brody warned me the cabin was empty."

"I'm not surprised. We're already here so we might as well check it out." Annette sidestepped Millie and opened the closet door. She stuck her head inside. "Empty."

"I'll take a quick look around the bathroom." Millie stepped up and into the compact space. She'd almost forgotten how small the crewmembers' cabins and bathrooms were, and her claustrophobia threatened to kick in.

She ignored her pounding heart as she eased the shower curtain aside and studied the interior.

Next up was a quick search of the corner medicine cabinet. She knelt down and ran her hand along the shelf below the sink. She even checked the small trash bin tucked in the corner.

Millie backed out of the bathroom. "The bathroom is clean."

Annette was inspecting the underside of the twin mattress. "I guess we should've known." She ran her hand along the base before lowering the mattress onto the bed.

"Annette." Millie's jaw dropped. "Check it out."

Chapter 10

Two inches from the bottom corner of the mattress was a gaping hole. "There's a hole in the wall."

"Literally." Annette leaned in for a closer inspection. "It looks like someone punched it."

Millie made a fist with her gloved hand and held it close to the jagged opening.

"Careful. There's a sharp piece of exposed steel." Annette studied the damaged wall. "Have you heard if Patterson or his men caught anything on the surveillance cameras?"

"Yeah. Whoever was with Wendy was careful to stay out of view. It had to have been someone familiar with the layout of the ship and position of the cameras." Millie straightened her back. "Let's say Wendy's attacker confronted her here inside the cabin. They became involved in some sort of physical altercation. The attacker/killer realized the cabin walls were paper-thin, and their argument could easily be overheard. They somehow tricked or convinced Wendy to meet them on the upper deck, in a private area and away from prying eyes and ears."

Annette picked up. "They argued again. The killer attacked, catching Wendy off guard and pushing her over the side of the ship. By the time the witness, who saw Wendy go over, made it up one deck to call for help, the killer was long gone."

Millie removed her cell phone from her pocket. She snapped several pictures of the hole in the wall while Annette scoured the rest of the small cabin.

"This must've been what Brody was trying not to tell me." Millie slipped her cell phone back in her pocket.

"A plausible conclusion or maybe nothing more than someone accidentally damaged the cabin wall."

Annette motioned to the door. "You ready to head out?"

"I'm sure Nic is beginning to wonder what happened to me." Millie eased the cabin door open. She peered into the hallway and could hear shoes squeaking on the polished concrete floor.

"Someone's coming." Millie hurriedly shut the door. She waited several long seconds before opening it again. The coast was clear. She motioned for Annette to hurry up and the women crept into the hall.

"Gloves." Annette held out her hand.

"Thanks for the loan." Millie slipped them off and handed them to her friend.

The women strode to the end of the hall. Millie rounded the corner first and collided head-on with Blackjack Blaze. Both of them took a quick step back.

"Blackjack."

"Millie Armati. I'm surprised to see you here in the crew cabin area at this hour of the night."

"I...uh."

Annette jumped in to help her. "Millie stopped by my cabin to get something. I don't believe we've met." She extended a hand. "I'm Annette Delacroix, Director of Food and Beverage on board this ship."

"Blackjack Blaze, entertainer extraordinaire."

"I'm sorry to hear about the unfortunate death of your assistant, Wendy Rainwell."

"I still can't believe Wendy is gone. Her family is on their way to Bermuda to retrieve her remains."

"I'm sure they're devastated." Millie thought about what Felix had told her earlier, how Blaze had posted a help-wanted ad for an assistant. She started to say something and then quickly changed her mind.

The ad could still be out there, and Millie wanted to see it. "It's a terrible tragedy," she agreed.

The women excused themselves, and Annette waited until they cleared the corridor and were a safe distance away. "Blackjack's cabin is near Wendy's cabin?"

"It's right next door."

"A convenient location if someone planned to confront Wendy without being seen," Annette pointed out.

"Yes, and that's not all." Millie told her friend how Felix mentioned Blackjack had placed an ad for an assistant on a cruise ship employment website.

"Does Patterson know?"

"I have no idea. I'll mention it to him tomorrow." Millie stifled a yawn. "Excuse me. I think it's time to hit the hay."

"I hear ya. Tomorrow is shaping up to be another busy day." Annette began making her way down the crew corridor while Millie turned toward the stairwell.

"Hey."

Annette turned back. "Yeah?"

"Are you going to talk to Amit? I know I already talked to him, but he was a little groggy."

"Sure. I'll do it first thing tomorrow morning. His shift starts at six."

"Do you mind if I stop by to hear what he has to say?"

"Mind?" Annette smiled. "I wouldn't expect anything less. Between the two of us, maybe we can help jog his memory."

Millie told her friend goodnight before climbing several sets of stairs until she reached the bridge. Nic stood talking to Myron Greaves, one of the ship's officers.

He gave Millie a wave. "I'll be along shortly."

"I'll be waiting." Millie never slowed and continued to their apartment where the lingering aroma of cinnamon greeted her.

She hung her lanyard on the hook near the door. "Scout, I'm home." She found the pup curled up on his doggie bed. "Hey, lazy bones."

Millie picked him up. "Would you like to go outside? First, I want to grab a snack." They circled through the kitchen. Annette's baked loaf of friendship bread...or what was left of it, sat on the counter.

Millie sliced a small piece and carried that, along with Scout, onto the balcony. It was a tasty morsel and she suddenly realized that other than grabbing the chicken Caesar wrap earlier, she'd skipped dinner.

She returned to the kitchen to grab a second slice when Nic wandered in. "The bread is good stuff."

"It's delicious," Millie mumbled through a mouthful.

"Did you tell Annette what I did?"

"No. I forgot." Millie motioned to what was left of the loaf. "Would you like a piece?"

"I thought you'd never ask." He watched his wife cut a generous slice and set it on a paper towel before handing both to him. "What did you have for dinner?"

"I grabbed a wrap earlier. It's been a busy day." Millie popped the last bite in her mouth and rinsed her hands in the kitchen sink. "How is the investigation into Wendy Rainwell's death going?"

"You mean you're not sticking your nose into this one?" her husband teased.

"Maybe, but I figured it wouldn't hurt to find out what Patterson's told you."

"There were some injuries sustained which may or may not have been related to Wendy's fall."

"And Amit is a suspect," Millie said. "He's a suspect since he was one of the last people seen talking to Wendy."

"I'm afraid so. He claims he was working at the time of the incident, which is true."

"So Amit is off the hook," Millie said.

"Not quite. His duties include checking on food stations all over the ship. He could've easily been in the vicinity of where she went overboard."

"Amit did not push Wendy overboard, nor did he cause any of her injuries. Patterson needs to take a closer look at the hole." As soon as the words were out of her mouth, Millie regretted her slip.

"Hole?" Nic lifted a brow. "What kind of hole?"

"I...uh. Annette and I took a quick look around Wendy's cabin. There was some damage to a wall," Millie blurted out. "No one told us we couldn't. Besides, Patterson had already removed all of her belongings."

"Millie Armati," Nic pointed his finger at his wife. "If Patterson finds out you've been snooping around, he's going to have your hide."

"It was only a quick look."

Nic shook his head and made his way out of the kitchen.

Millie hurried after him. "I can't stand by and let an innocent man - Amit - take the fall for Wendy's death. He didn't kill her. Blackjack Blaze is the real suspect."

Nic abruptly stopped. "What do you know about Blackjack Blaze?"

"I know he placed a help-wanted ad on a cruise ship employment site not long ago. Felix was the one who told me about it. He saw the ad."

"Was there anything else on the site?"

"I don't know. I haven't had a chance to log on and check it out."

"But you're going to," Nic guessed.

"I won't be breaking any laws."

Nic briefly closed his eyes. "I suppose. You told Patterson about the job posting?"

"Not yet. I haven't had time."

"I wonder why," her husband said sarcastically.

"You're angry with me because I'm trying to help a friend?"

Nic's tone softened and he reached for her hand. "Mad? No. Disappointed? Perhaps...but only because you're sticking your nose in where it doesn't belong, PLUS one of these days your meddling is going to come back to bite you."

"But not yet," Millie snuggled close to her husband. "I've been thinking about what you said earlier...on your way out of the past guest party. Is the offer still open?"

Nic let out a husky laugh. "You're trying to make me forget about your spying antics."

"Guilty as charged. You have to admit being distracted from my sleuthing sounds like a lot more fun," Millie teased.

"Now that you mention it." Nic placed his hands on his wife's hips and drew her close. "I think you should help me forget all about it."

Chapter 11

Nic was up and out of the apartment early the next morning to greet the harbor pilot and help guide the cruise ship into King's Wharf port.

Millie had spent half the night tossing and turning, wondering what Patterson had on Amit to bring him in for questioning a second time.

She was also champing at the bit to log onto the computer and research Blackjack Blaze. Because her husband left the apartment early, she took advantage of the few quiet moments to start her search.

First things first, she checked her email, the bank accounts and then got down to the business of finding out more about Blaze. She couldn't remember the name of the site Felix mentioned, but finally managed to locate it...Cruise Careers.

There were numerous positions available for entertainment jobs, and Millie finally gave up trying to find the one Felix mentioned. She wondered if perhaps Blackjack had removed the ad after Wendy's death, thinking it might look suspicious.

She logged off and then hustled around to get ready for work, leaving plenty of time to swing by the galley to see if Amit was available.

There were only a handful of early bird first shifters there when Millie arrived, and she found him prepping near the back.

"Hey, Amit."

"Miss Millie. You are up early today."

"I wanted to stop by to check on you. How are you feeling?" Millie stepped closer, noting the black circles under her friend's eyes.

"I...I'm okay. I'm still not sleeping, but after the scare the other day, I'm afraid to take anything." Amit chopped a head of lettuce in half and began dicing it. "Mr. Patterson is asking a lot of questions."

"About Wendy," Millie prompted.

"Yes."

"I feel somewhat responsible for the fact you're on Patterson's radar."

"You cannot blame yourself. You could not lie to Mr. Patterson. He is only doing his job." Amit explained again, how he met Wendy some months ago at Azure. "I remembered something else. When I first met Wendy, she was looking for another job."

"She was working for Blackjack Blaze?" Millie interrupted.

"Yes. She had only been with him for a short time. Wendy wanted to switch ships and had no control over where they went, so she was planning to part ways with Blaze."

Annette emerged from the storage area and joined them. "I thought I heard your voice."

"Nic started his shift early to greet the harbor pilot, so I figured I might as well start my day, too," Millie said. "I was just asking Amit about Wendy."

"I told Miss Millie I remembered something else. Wendy was looking for another job."

"Which fits in with what Felix told me," Millie said.

"Felix knew Wendy, too?" Amit's mouth dropped open.

"No. Blackjack Blaze posted Wendy's job on a cruise ship jobsite. Felix saw it not long ago. Tell me everything you know about Wendy's boyfriend."

"As I mentioned before, she told me his name was Jerry Dean. As soon as she tracked me down, I started asking other kitchen crewmembers in the crew galley and upstairs if they knew him."

"The more I think about it, the more I believe Wendy's boyfriend lied," Millie said.

Annette shoved her hand on her hip. "It's obvious the guy was feeding Wendy a line. He probably didn't even work in the kitchen or on board the ship."

"But he did work on the ship," Amit said. "Wendy watched him pass through security one night after he showed the guard his identification."

"You mentioned that before." Millie tapped her chin thoughtfully. "So we have two suspects. Blackjack Blaze, who was already looking for Wendy's replacement and she was looking for another job. We also have a mysterious boyfriend, Jerry Dean. I can run a check on him, but I'm sure there's no crewmember by that name."

"If what Wendy said was true, he's somewhere here on board our ship," Annette said. "We just have to figure out who he is."

"It will be like looking for a needle in a haystack."

"There is one more thing Wendy said." Amit glanced over his shoulder and lowered his voice.

"She made a comment she didn't think Jerry Dean would be thrilled to learn about the baby. Wendy hinted to him she was looking for a job on Siren of the Seas, and he tried to talk her out of it."

"Maybe because he had a girlfriend or was married?"

"Which would be a strong motivation to lie about his name," Annette replied.

Millie's radio began to squawk. "Millie, do you copy?"

It was Andy. She plucked the radio from her belt. "Go ahead, Andy."

"Where are you?"

"I'm in the galley."

"You haven't confirmed your schedule change."

"What schedule change?"

"The one I sent to your staff scheduler."

Millie's jacket pocket began to vibrate. "Hang on." She reached inside and pulled out the scheduler. "I...uh...must have missed it." She tapped the front of the screen to accept Andy's schedule change.

"Danielle isn't accepting her changes, either," Andy grumbled. "How can I test the reliability of the scheduler if you're ignoring it?"

"Maybe you should give them to someone else," Millie suggested.

"Very funny." Andy signed off, and Millie replaced her radio.

Annette pointed to the watch. "What is that?"

"It's SOSES. Siren of the Seas Entertainment Software." Millie handed the watch to her friend. "It works like an Apple wristwatch. It keeps the crews' schedules, and Andy can update it on the fly. It also comes with audio and visual features and Andy's favorite part - it'll scare you half to death."

Annette turned it over in her hand. "Very ingenious."

"If the trial run is successful, Andy plans to roll them out to all of the entertainment staff. For now, Danielle, Isla and I are the guinea pigs."

"What will they think of next?" Annette handed the watch back. "Are you getting off in Bermuda?"

"I have a couple of free hours, but nothing to do, so I think I'm going to stay on the ship." Millie consulted her new schedule. "I better get going. Andy will be down at the gangway waiting for me. According to the timer, I have less than a minute to make it to the atrium."

She darted to the door.

"Hey." Annette stopped her. "Are you keeping up with your friendship bread?"

"No." Millie grinned. "Nic baked it."

"Baked it?"

"I placed the final baking instructions on top of the bag. He thought he was doing me a favor by throwing it in the oven." Millie patted her stomach. "It was delicious. He added some cinnamon, chocolate chips and walnuts and then devoured most of it. There's only a small sliver left, which I'm sure will be long gone by the time I get home."

"Great," Annette grumbled. "You're gonna have to wait for another batch to finish its run before I can give you more."

"I'll take it. Nic will be thrilled." Millie gave her friend a small wave and hurried out of the galley. She made it to the gangway with a couple of seconds to spare.

"Right on time." Andy patted the watch.

"Were you able to track Danielle down?" Millie asked breathlessly.

"Yes. She said she put the watch in her pocket and forgot about it. I had to radio her, too. How can

I test these schedulers if I can't get you to use them?" he lamented.

"You need to figure out how to ditch the vibration."

The gangway was open for business, and the first round of passengers exited the ship. A family of four stopped by to ask for the back on board time.

Millie turned to Andy. "It's five today, isn't it?"

Andy pursed his lips and jabbed his finger at Millie's scheduler.

"Right." She quickly scrolled through the events. The print was small, and she tapped the screen to enlarge it. "All on board by five o'clock."

The man thanked Millie for the information, and they exited the ship.

"See how easy that was?" Andy asked. "All you have to do is check the scheduler."

"Yeah. I get the point." They stood there for another hour, seeing the passengers off before Andy consulted his scheduler. "I need to leave here shortly. I'm meeting with the captain and Donovan Sweeney to discuss Wendy's...departure. I gave you a couple of extra hours off this morning since I loaded you up the second half of the day."

"You did?" Millie scrolled through the screen, grudgingly admitting it was convenient to have everything up to date and at her fingertips. She almost told Andy but decided there were still some "bugs" he needed to work out before calling it a success.

"If you want to get off the ship, wander around the shopping area and stretch your legs, you'll have plenty of time."

"Thanks, Andy. That was very nice of you." Millie stayed behind to answer a few more questions before making her way upstairs to the gift shop.

Ocean Treasures was dark, but Millie caught a small movement in the back and spied the top of Cat's head. She rapped lightly on the window to get her attention.

Cat hurried over and unlocked the door. "Hey, Millie."

"Are you off today?"

"Until three o'clock when I'm heading down to the gangway to help security check packages. Why? What's up?"

"Andy gave me some time off this morning. I figured since the gift shop is closed while we're in port, you might want to get off for a few hours and have a look around."

Cat wrinkled her nose. "In Bermuda? I've been here before. There's nothing close to the port unless you're looking for touristy stuff." She could see a look of disappointment on Millie's face. "It's been a few years since I've been here. I'll go with you."

"Are you sure?" Millie's face lit.

"Yeah. I'm sure." Cat flung her arm around Millie's shoulders. "What could be better than spending time off with one of my besties? Speaking of friends, how are you doing with your friendship bread?"

"I'm not." Millie told Cat about Nic's helpful gesture.

She burst out laughing. "That's hilarious. And it tasted all right?"

"It was delicious. In fact, Nic enjoyed it so much; Annette is going to give me another batch when it's ready. I'm not sure it will make it all ten days before he decides to bake it again." Millie remembered the referral Gundervan had given to Annette and her recent bouts of distraction. "Has Annette said anything to you recently about her health?"

"No." Cat shook her head, a puzzled look on her face. "Is something wrong with Annette?"

"I...no. It's nothing." Millie decided to keep quiet. If...or when Annette had something to confide, she would. "I need to change before we head out."

She'd just turned to go when her radio went off. This time it was Danielle. "Where are you?"

"Cat and I are getting off the ship in a few. Do you want to go with us?"

"Nah. I'll pass. I think I'm gonna catch up on some rest. I need to talk to you. Call me on my cell phone."

"Will do." Millie replaced her walkie-talkie and dialed Danielle's cell phone. "What's up?"

"Are you going to keep an eye on Blaze?"

"Should I?"

"Maybe. Blaze and I originally planned to run through the show's routine this morning. He called a few minutes ago to say there was a change in plans, something suddenly came up, and he rescheduled."

"Interesting. I'll definitely keep an eye out for him." Millie thanked Danielle for the heads up and slipped her cell phone back in her pocket. "Can we walk to the shops?"

"I think so. If I remember correctly, there are some not far from the port."

"Perfect."

The women agreed to meet dockside in ten minutes, and Millie headed upstairs. It was a quick switch of clothing, and then she hurried down the gangway where Cat joined her moments later.

"Look at you." Millie pointed to the floppy straw hat, the rim trimmed in a coral floral pattern. Cat's pedal pushers matched the fabric of the hat. "All color coordinated and everything."

"I picked this up in Miami the other day. I figured I needed some new duds for our new adventure."

The women made their way along the side of the ship, through the security checkpoint and to Clocktower Mall. They meandered through several shops, stopping at one where Millie sampled the perfume while Cat purchased a "Bermuda Triangle" scarf.

They wandered through several more shops, and then Cat consulted her watch. "It's already two-thirty. I need to be back by three to help check bags."

The women began making their way to the ship when Millie recognized a familiar face. It was Blackjack Blaze, and he was heading in the opposite direction. She remembered Danielle's call, how Blaze had changed their plans because something had come up.

"Let's go." Millie grabbed her friend's arm and dragged her to the corner. She peered in the direction Blaze had gone, and could make out the tippy top of his head farther up the block.

"Where are we going?"

"We're following Blackjack Blaze." They continued walking at a brisk pace with Millie determined to keep a close eye on the man.

"Who is Blackjack Blaze?"

"Wendy Rainwell's boss. Wendy is the woman who went overboard."

Blackjack slowed his pace. Cat and Millie followed suit.

"Let's hang back." Millie craned her neck, her eyes never leaving Blackjack. "He's in a big hurry."

He crossed to the other side of the street, and Millie lost sight of him as a trolley rumbled past. "We lost him." She took off running.

"Wait for me!" Cat chased after her, catching up when Millie stopped at the corner.

"I knew it. I figured I was onto something."

Chapter 12

Millie pointed to Blackjack, who was standing on the other side of the street. He wasn't alone.

"Who is the other guy?" Cat asked.

"I don't know." Millie studied the man talking to Blackjack and spied a familiar lanyard hanging around his neck. "He works on board the ship. Do you recognize him, maybe someone who has stopped by the gift shop?"

Cat squinted her eyes. "No. I don't think so. He's not in uniform and wearing a ball cap, so it's hard to tell."

Millie removed her cell phone from her backpack and shifted to the side. She snapped a picture of the men. "They don't look happy."

"Nope. I wish we could hear what they're saying."

Blackjack turned to go. The man grabbed his arm, clenching his fist with his free hand.

"I think he's going to hit him."

Millie thought so, too. She sucked in a breath, waiting to see what happened next.

Blackjack jerked his arm from the man's grasp and stomped off. The other man, the crewmember, watched him go before slowly following behind.

"He's heading toward the ship." Millie hustled along the sidewalk, staying a few steps behind.

The unidentified crewmember passed through the security checkpoint. Millie darted to the gate and handed her ID to the port's security guard.

"Millie Armati?" He carefully inspected her card.

"Yes," she said impatiently.

"Your name sounds familiar."

"I'm the captain's wife."

"The captain's wife?" The guard chuckled. "Lucky you."

"I am." Millie pressed her palms together. "I'm sorry. I hate to be rude, but I'm kind of in a hurry."

"Sure." The guard handed her ID back. "Didn't mean to take up your time."

"No. I mean it's fine," Millie apologized. "I'm sorry." She picked up the pace, hurrying down the dock to the crew gangway, but it was too late. The man who had been talking to Blackjack was already back on board the ship and long gone. "The man who just passed through...do you know his name?"

The gangway security guard shook his head. "What man?"

"The man who just came through here. Can you check for me?"

He eyed Millie suspiciously. "No. We're not allowed to do that."

Someone nudged her in the back in an attempt to get her to keep moving. Millie reluctantly placed her backpack on the scanner. It rolled through, and she grabbed it on the other side as she waited for Cat to join her. "He got away."

"Security can't identify him?" Cat asked.

"Can, but won't," Millie grumbled.

"At least you snapped a picture of him. It's only a matter of time before you figure out who he is. I better go change." Cat lifted the bag containing the scarf. "Thanks for inviting me to go with you today. I had fun."

"So did I. Maybe on our next stop, Nic and I can explore the island. It looks nice."

Cat headed to her cabin while Millie climbed the stairs. When she reached the apartment, she followed Scout out onto the balcony and then turned her cell phone on so she could study the picture.

The men were definitely having a serious conversation. Her first thought was to show the picture to Amit and Annette to see if either of them recognized him.

The intense midday sun beat down on the balcony, and Scout didn't waste any time taking care of business before returning to the cool air conditioned apartment.

Millie checked his food and water before heading to the galley. It was a madhouse. Identifying the man would have to wait.

First up was a round of trivia, followed by a cooking class with Massimo Ricci, the Italian Michelin chef, where they were making homemade pizza from scratch. The handful of participants added the ingredients for the dough and mixed it together. Millie began kneading hers as she mulled over Wendy's death.

Perhaps Blackjack was responsible for Wendy's death. He was searching for a new assistant. There was a reason he never mentioned the job posting.

Maybe he was concerned he wouldn't get the job on board the ship if Andy thought he was looking for help.

There was also the mysterious man Blackjack met with earlier. Could it have been Wendy's boyfriend? If so, why hadn't Blackjack named him as a suspect? She thought about the suspicious hole in Wendy's cabin wall.

Millie dusted the flour from her hands and pulled her cell phone from her pocket. She enlarged the picture of the men and studied their hands. She wasn't certain, but neither appeared to be injured.

"Are we not working on our creation?" Ricci clapped his hands to get Millie's attention.

She fumbled with the phone, nearly dropping it in the bowl of pizza dough. "Sorry."

They finished rolling out the dough and began working on balls of mozzarella. The group then set them aside and started preparing the pizza sauce.

Millie sampled her sauce several times before creating what she deemed the perfect blend of tomatoes and Italian spices.

Once the pizza dough, the balls of mozzarella and the sauce were finished, the assembly was a snap. She sparingly added chunks of cheese and strategically placed slices of tomatoes before topping it with a generous amount of fresh basil.

The pies were placed inside the oven and then Ricci made his rounds, thanking them for attending his class and presenting each of them with a special chef's hat. He handed Millie her hat. "You are a natural, Millie."

"At making pizza?" She smiled in amusement. "Don't sign me up as a sous chef anytime soon."

"You are enjoying our long voyage?"

"So far, so good. You must be thrilled the ship is heading back toward home."

"I am. I will be taking a couple of weeks off next month to visit family."

The chef moved on and continued chatting with the guests. Millie worked the crowd in the opposite direction, attempting to get a feel for how the class went so she could report back to Andy.

After the pizzas finished cooking, Millie sampled hers and then placed the leftovers in a to-go container for Nic.

Before heading home, she decided to stop by the galley again. It was mid-afternoon, and the kitchen was quiet.

Amit was nowhere in sight. Annette was in the corner, chatting with a handful of her kitchen crew. The conversation ended, and she joined her friend. "How was Bermuda?"

"I enjoyed getting off the ship and stretching my legs. Cat and I didn't venture beyond the shops in the port area."

"Shopping?" Annette wrinkled her nose. "I can think of a million things I would rather do than shop."

"Check this out." Millie removed her phone from her pocket. She switched it on and swiped the screen until she found the picture of Blackjack and the unidentified man. "Do you recognize this man?"

"Which one?"

"The shorter one, the one wearing the ball cap."

Annette silently studied the picture and then slowly shook her head. "No. Who's the other guy?"

"Blackjack Blaze. He's kind of far away, so it's hard to see. Cat and I caught them talking. I thought I might be onto something if he was a kitchen employee."

"Or a cruise ship employee," Annette said.

"He's a ship employee. He's wearing a lanyard."

"You're right. I see it now." Annette handed the phone back. "You think this guy might be Wendy's boyfriend, Jerry Dean?"

"It's possible." Millie glanced around. "Is Amit here? Maybe he'll recognize the guy."

"He's taking care of some room service deliveries for me. We're a little short-staffed today. He should be back in about an hour."

"I'll be working." Millie snapped her fingers. "Wait a minute. Danielle and Blackjack are meeting soon to begin practicing for their show tonight. Maybe I should just ask him."

"Why not?" Annette shrugged. "At the very least, you'll catch him off guard."

"My thoughts exactly."

*****

The theater seating area was dark, but front and center was the opposite with bright spotlights illuminating the stage. Blackjack and Danielle were both there, along with several others.

Millie slipped into an empty seat. She could tell from the scowl on Danielle's face she was irritated.

"Could you at least try to look a smidgen happy?" Blackjack pleaded.

"I'm not happy. I don't like crowds. I'm already itching, and I don't even have the stupid dress on. I'm having visions of crashing to the floor in those ridiculously high heels, and then I'll be the laughingstock of the entire ship."

Millie popped out of her seat and approached the edge of the stage. "Danielle. It's only for a few nights. Surely, you can fake it."

"Fake it 'til you make it," Blackjack quipped.

"Andy will owe you one," Millie sing-songed.

"You're right." Danielle brightened at the thought. "He'll definitely owe me one."

The two flew through the practice. Blackjack ended his performance with a low bow and turned to his assistant. "You were not bad for your first try."

"*Not bad*? Go find someone else who's better."

"I meant it as a compliment." Blackjack thanked her. "I'll see you at five forty-five backstage to get ready for a final run through, this time with another set of illusions."

"Great." Danielle tromped down the stage steps and joined Millie. "How was Bermuda?"

"Cat and I did a little shopping. It was nice to get off the ship, although we didn't have a lot of time." Millie cast a quick glance at Blackjack, who was wheeling his magic cart off the stage.

"Hang on." Millie sidestepped her friend and darted up the steps. "Blackjack."

The man waited for Millie to join him. "Yes?"

"You got off the ship earlier."

"I did." Blackjack nodded. "I met with Wendy's family, to offer my condolences. It was a heartbreaking meeting."

"I'm sure it was. My friend and I got off the ship, too. We did some shopping."

"I see." Blackjack's eyes glazed over and he shifted impatiently.

"I saw you in town." Millie hurried on. "You were talking to another of the ship's employees. I was going to say hello, but I didn't want to interrupt your conversation."

Blackjack straightened his back. "I don't know what you're talking about. I didn't meet anyone off the ship other than Wendy's family. You must have me confused with someone else."

Millie reached for her phone, to show him the proof, how she'd snapped a picture of him and the other man, but quickly changed her mind. Blackjack Blaze was lying.

Chapter 13

"It was probably just someone who bore a striking resemblance to you," Millie mumbled.

Blackjack nodded, and the cart rumbled out of sight.

Danielle grabbed Millie's arm. "He's lying?"

"Without a doubt." Millie handed her friend her phone.

"That's definitely Blaze. I don't recognize the other guy."

"Me, either. I need to show the picture to Amit."

Millie and Danielle parted ways in the hall with Millie once again returning to the galley. Amit wasn't around, and this time neither was Annette.

She turned to go and collided head-on with her friend who barreled through the swinging door.

"Sorry," Annette grabbed Millie's arm. "I didn't mean to bulldoze over the top of you."

"No problem. It seems like I'm hanging around here a lot lately. You're probably getting tired of seeing me."

"Nah." Annette waved dismissively. "I know you're trying to help Amit, and we both appreciate it."

"Speaking of Amit, I thought I would stop by to see if he was back yet. Blackjack claims he never met with anyone in port, other than Wendy's family."

"So maybe the guy in the photo is a member of the family."

"I suppose." Millie frowned. "I hadn't considered that angle, although he was wearing a crewmember lanyard."

"Amit's having a rough day. He and Carlah got into an argument. She heard a rumor that Wendy and Amit were close friends and is accusing him of cheating on her."

"Poor guy. He can't catch a break." Millie patted her pocket. "I need to figure out who's in the picture with Blackjack. He's definitely a crewmember and on board this ship."

"That's it." Annette snapped her fingers. "All you gotta do is take a look at the crew tracking system, figure out who boarded the ship and dinged their keycard around the time the mystery employee boarded."

"Annette," Millie beamed. "You're brilliant."

Her enthusiasm was short-lived. "I tried to get the guard at the gangway to tell me his name when I boarded and he refused. I can't think of a single person in security who'll give me access to the employee tracking program so I can check the records."

"There has to be a way." Annette eyed her friend thoughtfully. "I know someone who *might* be able to sneak through the computer's back door and access the crew tracking system."

"Who?"

"No." Annette shook her head. "Forget I said anything."

"C'mon Annette. Who is it?"

"All right. It's Sharky."

"Sharky?" Millie lifted a brow. "Sharky can find out which employees boarded the ship and the exact time?"

"Well..." Annette's eyes slid to the side. "When we went on our non-date, he was bragging about how he's some sort of computer whiz and figured out a way to access all of the restricted computer software. He didn't tell me he could access the employee gangway entries but it's possible. It's also possible he was just blowing smoke and doesn't have a clue."

"True."

"If he wasn't making it up, he might be your best shot at taking a look at the boarding records. You'll have to be exact on the time." Annette gave her friend a thumbs up. "I say go for it. Good luck."

"What do you mean, 'good luck?' Aren't you going with me? I'm doing this for you - for Amit."

"You know how I feel about Sharky."

"And I know how he feels about you. If anyone can convince Sharky to help, it's you."

Annette stubbornly shook her head. "I'll whip up his favorite foods. I'll do whatever I can to get him to agree to help, anything but show up on his doorstep. He's been backing off lately, and I don't want to give him a smidgen of false hope." She headed toward the large walk-in cooler, and Millie followed her.

"I can go by myself, but I know what he's going to say. He's going to ask about you."

Annette ignored Millie and began sorting through the cartons of dairy products.

"You're serious. You're not going to help me try to clear Amit's name?"

"I am helping. I just gave you a great idea." Annette grabbed a container of whipped cream and carried it out of the cooler.

Millie's attempt to convince Annette to accompany her was futile. "Fine. I'll head down there by myself, but I'll be lucky if he agrees to help."

"Sharky is a negotiator. All you have to do is reach a mutual agreement."

"This oughta be interesting."

"Good luck."

Millie stepped out of the galley and strolled to the aft before taking the stairs to the maintenance deck. All the while, she tried to come up with a plan to entice Sharky to help her. The only two things that interested the maintenance supervisor were Annette and food, both of which tied in together.

Millie reached the maintenance office and could hear Sharky's voice through the open door. "That's it. Now get outta here and get back to work."

She made a hasty retreat, clearing the doorway only seconds before several maintenance workers stampeded out, leaving Sharky and Reef, the other maintenance supervisor, alone inside.

The men stood close together, talking in low voices.

Millie cleared her throat, and Reef was the first to notice her. "Hey, Millie."

"Hi, Reef. I'm sorry to interrupt. I can come back later."

"Nah," Sharky said. "We were wrapping up. Reef is leaving."

"Don't forget what I said about the boss man. You better come up with a way to explain the missing case of beef jerky, or it's back on probation." Reef made a slicing motion across his neck.

"I told you I would take care of it, and I will."

Reef eased past Millie on his way out.

Sharky plopped down in his office chair. "What brings you back to my neck of the woods?"

Millie got right to the point. "Word on the street is you may have access to the computer program that tracks keycard swipes when employees are boarding or leaving the ship. I need to track down a record from earlier today."

"I might be able to help." Sharky plucked an unlit cigar from his pocket and shoved it in his mouth as he eyed Millie with interest. "What's in it for me?"

Millie eased into an empty chair. "You tell me."

"Well..." Sharky's chair creaked loudly as he leaned back and stared up at the ceiling. "Good grub is always appreciated." He eased the chair upright. "How's Annette?"

"Busy."

"Aren't we all?" Sharky resumed his position as he eyed the ceiling. "Before we begin negotiations, I need a little more information."

"What kind of information?"

"Why do you need to access the gangway records?"

"Because a friend is being questioned in Wendy Rainwell's death, and I'm trying to help clear his name." Millie wasn't sure how much she should divulge and then decided to plow ahead. "I think Blackjack Blaze, Wendy's boss, may be involved. I saw him talking to a ship employee earlier today in Bermuda. I followed the man back on board but before I could catch up with him, he disappeared. Blackjack denied meeting him. There's something up, and I need to figure out who he was talking to."

"I see." Sharky lowered his gaze and studied Millie. "So this Blackjack guy met with someone off the ship, you saw them together and he denied it."

"In a nutshell. The mystery employee swiped his card less than five minutes before I swiped mine, which narrows down the timeline of records I need to access."

Sharky pressed the tips of his fingers together. "I don't plan on it, but if I get caught accessing the security records, I...we could find ourselves in big trouble."

"You're right," Millie agreed.

"So...if I'm going to stick my neck out there, I need to make it worth my while...*really* worth my while."

"What do you want?" Millie asked bluntly.

"I need a favor...or more like favors in the form of a double dipper."

"Double dipper?"

"Two favors," Sharky confirmed. "Are you interested in negotiating?"

"Possibly. I need to know what I'm doing in exchange for you snooping," Millie said.

"Number one, I need Cat to deep-six her claim about a missing case of Jack Link's beef jerky. She needs to write it off as a loss."

"You 'borrowed' a case of jerky," Millie clarified. "Cat filed a report for missing product. It was traced back to you."

"In a roundabout way."

"Why don't you just return it?"

Sharky rubbed his protruding stomach. "The jerky is long gone."

"I see. Moving on...what is your second demand?"

"Not a demand. I like to think of it as more of you scratch my back, I'll scratch yours."

"Call it whatever you want. What's number two on your list?"

"I need some time off when we reach Southampton."

"Time off is approved by your supervisor."

"I've already put my request in," Sharky said. "Sweeney is dragging his feet. I think it has something to do with the missing jerky, but I can't be certain."

"What would a case of missing beef jerky have to do with getting time off?" Millie asked.

"Well." Sharky rubbed the stubble on his chin. "It's not the first time a box of goods has gone missing while passing through my loading dock. Sweeney's cranked up about this one for some reason and is throwing around the word probation."

"So you want me to try to get approval for time off in exchange for taking a quick look at the security records from earlier today."

"You're one smart cookie, Millie. Do we have a deal? We can get on it right now if we can reach a verbal agreement."

"You don't want me to sign my name in blood?" Millie joked.

"Very funny." Sharky leaned forward eagerly. "So?"

There was a fifty/fifty chance she wouldn't be able to persuade Donovan to allow Sharky time off. Another thought occurred to her. "What's the big deal with you getting off in Southampton?"

"I'm meeting someone."

"Meeting someone?" Millie's interest was piqued. "Who are you meeting?" She could tell from the look on Sharky's face that he was growing uncomfortable with this line of questioning.

"Nobody you know."

"This must be a pretty big deal for you. The only things you've ever been interested in are food and Annette."

He squirmed when she mentioned Annette's name, and it dawned on her. "You're meeting a woman in Southampton."

"Maybe." Sharky glanced at his watch. "What is this...twenty questions? I need to get back to work. If you want to check the records, we're running out of time."

Millie paused. "We may have a deal if you tell me who you're so gung-ho to meet in the UK."

"Geez," Sharky grunted. "Fine. Her name is Svetlana. I met her on a Russian dating site. We're meeting in person in Southampton. Are you happy?"

"You met a woman from another country online?"

"Yes, and we hit it off from the moment we started chatting."

"You haven't sent her money, have you? This could be a scam."

"It's not a scam," Sharky insisted. "She's legit."

"I hope you know what you're getting yourself into," Millie shook her head. "Let's quickly recap our agreement. You need me to ask Cat to write off the case of missing jerky and also see if I can convince Donovan to give you time off the day we dock in Southampton in exchange for accessing the gangway records."

"You got it." Sharky eagerly extended a hand. "Do we have a deal?"

Chapter 14

"I'm concerned about you stealing..."

"Not stealing, permanently borrowing," Sharky interrupted.

"Fine. Permanently borrowing stuff from the store. Despite my reservations, I believe there may be a way to resolve your dilemma." Millie shook Sharky's hand. "We have a deal."

Sharky sprang from his chair and waltzed over to the office door. He yanked it open and then peered out, looking both ways. "Coast is clear."

Millie watched him close the door and turn the lock. "You're locking us in?"

"This is top-secret stuff. If we get caught, borrowing beef jerky and being on probation will look like child's play."

"But we're not stealing anything, we're just looking around."

"Then why don't you use your hubby's computer? I'm sure he has access to the same records and more."

"He does." Millie glanced at her hands. "I promised Nic I wouldn't access restricted information on our computer."

"But you're okay if I do it," Sharky said.

"We have an agreement. Besides, you assured me we weren't going to get caught."

"I'll try my best." Sharky sat on the edge of his office chair and adjusted his keyboard. "You say there's a limited timeframe we need to check."

"Yes." Millie grew silent as she tried to remember the exact time. "I remember Cat had to be back on board by three. We had less than half an hour to spare. Maybe around two forty-five?"

"That's a start." Sharky tapped the keys. "I see your return time. It was at approximately two forty-seven this afternoon."

"So back up a few minutes. It would have been somewhere between two forty and two forty-five."

Sharky scrolled through the screen. "Five employee keycards were dinged during that five-minute timeframe."

Millie slid forward in her chair. "Can you jot down the names?"

"I can do one better." The portable printer behind him started to whir and then spit out a single sheet of paper.

Sharky snatched it off the printer and waved it in the air. "Here's the printout."

"Sweet." Millie reached for it. "This was easier than I thought it would be."

Sharky held it over his head. "Ah. Ah. Ah. Not so fast."

"We had a deal."

"We *have* a deal. I held up my end of the bargain. Now it's time for you to take care of yours."

"I promised. I gave you my word," Millie said.

Sharky dangled the sheet of paper in his hand.

"Come on," Millie said. "Have I ever let you down?"

"I never did get a second date with Annette."

"And I never promised you one. Besides, you have Swetvana now."

"Svetlana," Sharky corrected.

"Give me the paper. On my next break, I'll stop by Donovan's office to present your case for him giving you time off."

"Today?"

"Yes. Today."

"What time will I have my answer?" Sharky persisted.

193

"Before eleven tonight." Millie wasn't sure she could deliver on the requested time off, but she had promised him she would try, and she planned to keep her promise.

"And the beef jerky?"

"I'll chat with Cat as soon as I leave here."

Finally satisfied with Millie's answers, Sharky handed her the paper.

Millie glanced at the list of names before folding the sheet in thirds. "I'll get back with you before the end of the day."

He popped out of his chair and followed Millie to the door. "Don't forget about me. I'll be waiting."

"I'm sure you will." Millie thanked him before making her way up the stairs to deck seven. Ocean Treasures was dark and the shop was closed. She remembered Cat telling her she was filling in near the gangway, checking bags for security.

She found her friend near the scanner, chatting with a crewmember. Millie caught her eye, and Cat made her way over. "Did you find anything out?"

"Annette didn't recognize the employee. She suggested a way for me to get my hands on the names of the crewmembers who returned around the same time we did." Millie lowered her voice. "I have the list, but haven't had time to look at it yet."

"Cool," Cat said. "How did you get a list? That's restricted information."

"It is. You probably don't want to know." Millie changed the subject. "I need a favor."

Cat lifted a brow. "A favor?"

"There's a certain case of beef jerky, designated for the ship's store which went missing in Miami."

"Yes. I was the one who reported it missing. Do you know how expensive jerky is?"

"I know it's pricey," Millie agreed. "You're not going to get it back."

"Someone ate it," Cat guessed.

"Bingo."

Cat's eyes narrowed. "Sharky. Sharky put you up to this."

"He did me a favor. In exchange, I agreed to try to negotiate some sort of resolution."

"That jerk."

"I don't blame you for being upset, and I'm not on board with him stealing the jerky. There has to be another way...what about an IOU?"

"I suppose we can work out some sort of agreement, a payment plan." Cat tapped her toe on the floor. "So Sharky was able to provide you with records on employee keycard swipes in exchange for resolving my case of the missing jerky."

"That about sums it up."

"What a sneaky snake. Tell him to stop by the store sometime tomorrow to fill out a payroll deduction form."

"I will." Millie patted her friend's arm. "Thanks for helping me out."

"You're welcome." Cat returned to her spot near the bag checker and Millie headed upstairs to join Andy to greet returning passengers.

The duo fielded a range of questions before Andy finally excused himself. Millie stayed behind to wait for the last few stragglers to board and Suharto ordered the gangway pulled.

The ship began drifting away from the dock, and the realization they would be at sea for several long days before reaching the Azores began sinking in. "Here we go."

She waited until the shoreline disappeared before passing by the guest services desk. Millie caught a glimpse of Donovan Sweeney talking with one of the employees. Remembering her promise to Sharky, she clenched her jaw, and with determined steps, approached the counter.

Donovan finished his conversation and made his way over. "Hello, Millie."

"Hi, Donovan. I wondered if you had a moment."

"Of course."

"I have a favor to ask."

"A favor?" Donovan eyed her curiously. "Let's chat in my office."

Millie swung the half door open and followed Donovan inside.

"How are you enjoying our voyage so far?"

"Wendy Rainwell's death was a sad start to the trip."

"Yes, it was." Donovan sank into his chair on the other side of the desk. "Patterson stopped by earlier. He met with Wendy's family. They're taking her death hard."

"I'm sure they are. I don't think it was an accident or that she intentionally jumped."

"So, you've been doing a little digging around?" Donovan leaned back in his chair.

"Maybe. I know better than to step on Patterson's toes. I'm trying to keep my nose out of it...as much as possible, except for the fact my good friend, Amit Uddin, is a suspect."

"Amit is a good man, a hard worker. I'm sure it's only a matter of time before Patterson clears him."

"I hope so."

Donovan grew silent as he studied Millie's face and she started to squirm.

"So, what's the favor?"

"It's for a friend. Sharky Kiveski. He's hoping for some time off when the ship reaches Southampton. He told me he's still waiting for you to approve it."

"You're friends with Sharky?" Donovan chuckled. "Are you sure we're talking about the same person?"

"We've gotten to know each other over the past couple of years. He dated Annette."

"Annette Delacroix?" Donovan's jaw dropped. "You're joking."

"No, it's not a joke and it was only one date. They're not an item, and a bit of advice...you probably don't want to mention it to her. It's kind of a sore spot."

"So Sharky asked you, as a favor, to see if you could convince me to give him time off when the ship docks in Southampton?"

"Yes." Millie decided elaborating on the reason might boost Sharky's case. "He's been chatting with a woman online. He plans to meet her in person when we dock. Her name is Svet-something. Svetlana or Swetlana. She's Russian."

"A Russian blind date?" Donovan doubled over, roaring with laughter. "He's asking for trouble."

"I told him the same thing," Millie said quietly, "but he's determined."

"If anyone deserves a Russian blind date, it's Sharky." Donovan's laughter subsided, and he swiped at his eyes. "You know what, Millie? I think Sharky should meet this woman, so I'm going to say 'yes.' Definitely, yes."

"He hopes to meet her the first day, the day we dock."

Donovan opened his desk drawer, reached inside and pulled out a file folder. He flipped it open, grabbed a pen and began writing.

Millie watched him fill out the form and sign the bottom.

"There." Donovan handed Millie the top sheet. "I've given Sharky from five p.m. until midnight off the day we arrive."

"For real?" Millie took a quick glance at the paper and then stood. "Thank you, Donovan. I mean, thank you from Sharky."

"Promise me one thing," Donovan said.

"Sure."

"I want to know how the date turns out."
Donovan burst out laughing again. He was still
laughing as Millie made her way out of his office.

She carefully placed Sharky's time off approval
form in her pocket, next to the printout Sharky had
given her, and then made her way upstairs to check
on Scout.

Nic was still on the bridge with the King's Wharf
harbor pilot, so Millie kept going. She let Scout out
onto the balcony and pulled Sharky's printout from
her pocket. She slipped her reading glasses on and
scanned the sheet.

There were two female names and three male
crewmembers on the list. Kimel Pang was one of
them. Millie immediately dismissed him. Kimel was
the head of housekeeping.

Next on the list was Bartrand Melbane. The name
didn't ring a bell, and Millie had no idea who he
was.

The third name on the sheet was a male employee who returned to the ship at precisely two forty-four p.m.

Chapter 15

"Justin Fleming," Millie whispered. "Why does that name sound familiar?" She racked her brain trying to figure out who the man was but finally gave up. Perhaps she had heard the name in passing.

She made a mental note to run both names by Annette, to see if either of them rang a bell. "C'mon, Scout."

Scout trotted back inside the apartment and sat staring up at her, a sad expression on his face.

"Would you like to hang out with me for a couple of hours?" Millie consulted her wristwatch. Her next event didn't start until after the dinner hour.

She reached for her radio. "Danielle, do you copy?" Millie tried a couple of times before Danielle finally replied.

"Hey, Millie."

"What time are you and Blackjack running through the final practice before tonight's show?"

"Now."

"You're practicing now?"

"You could say that." Danielle sighed heavily. "Let's put it this way. I'm here. Blackjack is setting up."

"I'm on my way...to give you moral support."

"I need all of the help I can get."

Millie clipped the radio on her belt before scooping Scout up. "Shall we go cheer Danielle on?"

They made it as far as the theater doors before a couple stopped them to greet Scout.

"What a cute pup," the woman gushed.

"His name is Scout." Millie shifted the dog so the woman could pet him.

"I didn't know pets were allowed on board," the man chimed in.

"They're not, but the captain made an exception." Millie didn't mention the captain was her husband or that the dog belonged to them. They made small talk about the port day and dogs, and then she excused herself.

Millie and Scout joined Andy, who stood at the bottom of the steps.

"Danielle said you were stopping by to offer moral support." Andy patted Scout's head. "Had any good zaps lately?"

"No. Now that you mention it."

"Good," Andy beamed. "I did a little tweaking. Your alerts should come via a small chime. Now that you're here, we can test it out."

Andy whipped his cell phone from his pants pocket. His brow furrowed as he focused on the screen.

TING.

Millie jumped at the loud chime, tightening her grip on Scout.

Andy's eyes grew wide. "A little too loud?"

"A little. It's better than the shock, but not by much."

Andy tapped the screen again, and the watch chimed softly.

"Perfect." Millie dismissed the new notification. "I think you've finally got it."

Clomp. Clomp. Danielle clomped across the stage, her high heels rapping sharply on the stage floor.

Millie grinned.

"It's not funny," Danielle fumed. "The stupid outfit is bunching up in the back." She reached behind her and began tugging on the spaghetti straps.

"Be careful," Andy said. "That dress is worth a month's salary."

"You paid too much." Danielle released her grip on the delicate strap. "I need a massive pay raise for participating in these shenanigans."

Blackjack clapped his hands and began tugging a portable fish tank filled with water behind him. "Enough small talk. It's time to get to work." He placed it in the center of the stage and motioned for Danielle to join him.

She marched across the stage, a surly expression firmly in place.

"Danielle," Andy warned.

"Fine." Danielle forced a smile.

Blackjack reached under the cabinet and handed her a smaller, empty fish bowl. "If my lovely assistant, Danielle, would do me the honor of holding this fish bowl." He handed the bowl to her.

"Pay close attention to this amazing illusion." Blackjack unbuttoned the sleeves on his shirt and began rolling them up.

Next, he scooped a handful of water from the larger tank. He dumped the water into Danielle's smaller, empty bowl. Instead of water, a silver dollar hit the bottom of the bowl with a *clank*.

"Huh?" Danielle's jaw dropped as she stared at the coin in the bottom of the bowl.

"It's magic." Blackjack scooped water and dropped a second coin into the smaller bowl. The scoop and drop continued until a layer of coins filled the bottom.

"And now for the real trick. May I?" Blackjack motioned to the bowl, and Danielle handed it to him.

The magician dumped the coins back into the larger fish tank, but instead of silver dollars, a school of goldfish appeared.

Danielle clapped her hands. "That was amazing. How did you do that?"

Blackjack smiled widely, revealing an even set of pearly whites. "I did it really well."

Andy chuckled, and he and Millie began clapping. "Bravo. The passengers will love the trick."

"What did the fish say when he posted bail?' Blackjack asked. "I'm off the hook." He tapped his foot on the floor. "Da-da-da-dum."

The man was on a roll. "What do you get when you cross a banker with a fish? A loan shark." Blackjack rattled off a few more corny jokes before beginning another magic trick, this one involving a flamethrower.

He wowed the trio with another round of illusions, followed by a few one-liners and then the practice show ended.

Millie sprang to her feet and began clapping. "That was awesome. The fish tank and coin trick was my favorite, but the flame thrower will get the crowds going, too."

Andy stepped onto the stage and slapped Blackjack on the back. "Well done, old chap. We'll run through this show twice tonight and then again toward the end of the cruise."

"I have another routine we need to run through," Blackjack said.

Danielle shook her head. "But not today."

"Not today," Blackjack agreed.

"I'm going to head back to the dressing room to psych myself into tonight's performance." Danielle lifted the hem of her skirt and began making her way backstage.

Millie and Scout hurried after her. They caught up with Danielle in the dressing room. "You did great. It's going to be an awesome show."

"Thanks. I'll be glad when it's over. This isn't my thing."

"Even Scout thinks you did a great job." Millie placed the teacup Yorkie on the makeup counter, and he trotted to Danielle's side.

"Maybe you should do the show." Danielle gently picked him up and began cooing. "You're much cuter than me."

"I know you hate dressing up, but you're smokin' hot in that dress."

"I would much rather be in uniform." Danielle changed the subject. "Did you track down Amit and Annette?"

"I did one better. I got a list of names, of the employees who boarded the ship around the same time I did. I think one of them may be the person I caught Blackjack talking with in port." Millie removed the printout Sharky had given her from her pocket. "Do the names Bartrand Melbane or Justin Fleming ring a bell?"

Danielle thought about it for a moment. "Nope."

"Why would Blackjack lie about meeting this guy?" Millie waved the paper in the air. "What if one of these is the man Wendy was searching for?"

Danielle set Scout on the counter and patted his head. "It should be fairly easy to figure out."

"The only problem is...I'm exhausting my resources. I've already asked Sharky who, by the way, knows his way around the ship's restricted computer access programs, to help me."

"He's the one who gave you this sheet?" Danielle shook her head. "Somehow, I'm not surprised. He could probably tell you where these guys work."

"I don't want to ask him for help again."

"You could easily log onto your computer and figure it out."

"Except I promised Nic I wouldn't access restricted information on our home computer."

Danielle snapped her fingers. "What about Cat? She has access to that information, the names and even the cabin numbers of all employees because of the online charging system."

"You're right." Millie squeezed Danielle's arm. "Why didn't I think of that? I owe you one."

"Great. You can fill in for me tonight," Danielle joked.

"Very funny." Millie picked Scout up and headed toward the door. "I'm going to swing by the gift shop right now and ask her to check into it. I'll be back later to catch the show."

"Thanks. Maybe I can convince Blackjack to swap out one of the magic tricks and make me disappear instead."

"You'll be fine." Millie hurried across the stage, down the steps and out of the theater. She had enough time to swing by Ocean Treasures, and then return Scout to the apartment before her evening lineup.

She was halfway to the gift shop when her wristwatch chimed. "Now what? Andy Walker. What have you gotten me into this time?"

Chapter 16

"Senior Singles Mix and Mingle." Millie reached for her radio. "Andy Walker, do you copy?"

"Go ahead, Millie," Andy's voice boomed.

"What's this 'Senior Singles Mix and Mingle?'"

"The regular mix and mingles tends to attract the younger crowd, so I figured I would test a new singles gathering for our fifty-five and up passengers. I planned to host it myself, but something came up so I need you to fill in."

"I better get a move on. I've got twenty minutes to run an errand, drop Scout off at home and hightail it to Marseille Lounge."

"Isn't this new scheduling app working great?" Andy gushed.

"Yeah. It's great," Millie muttered. "I can't wait to see what you dream up next." She signed off and then replaced her radio, casting a longing glance in the direction of the gift shop. There wasn't enough time to research the two male crewmembers, take Scout home and make it to her next event.

She hustled onto the bridge where First Officer Craig McMasters and another officer were working. She greeted both but didn't slow as she continued making her way to the apartment.

The door was ajar. "Hello? Nic?"

"In here," he called out.

The crisp, cool air conditioning and the earthy citrus smell of her husband's cologne greeted her. Nic stepped into view, and she let out a low whistle. "Look at you all dressed up and ready to paint the town...or should I say, paint the ship."

Nic tugged on his collar. "Andy convinced me to make an appearance at a senior mingles get-together."

"I'm going, too." Millie stepped close to her husband, closing her eyes as she breathed in his cologne. "And I am one lucky woman."

"You'll be joining me?" Nic wrapped his arms around his wife and pulled her closer. "This is the best news I've had all day."

"I couldn't agree more." Millie took a step back. "Let me freshen up and we'll go together."

"I'll take Scout out while I wait." Nic and Scout headed onto the balcony while Millie darted up the stairs. She smoothed her hair and spritzed Nic's favorite perfume on before returning to the living room where he stood waiting. He extended his arm. "Shall we?"

Millie slipped her arm through her husband's arm, and they exited the apartment. Nic gave the other officers a jaunty wave as the couple passed through the bridge.

Marseille Lounge was packed. Nic led his wife past several of the attendees, making their way to the front of the room. Millie stepped onto the stage to address the guests and then introduced her husband to a rousing round of applause.

Nic greeted the passengers before rattling off the ship's position, the weather for the rest of the evening and the estimated arrival time in the Azores while servers circled the room offering the guests beverages.

Several more servers were on hand with trays of hors d'oeuvre. "Mrs. Armati?"

Millie inspected the offerings. "These all look divine. What do we have?"

The server shifted the tray and pointed to a toasted cracker. "This is crab on an avocado toast. It's a combination of sweet crabmeat tossed with fresh mint and lime juice."

Millie's mouth watered. She reached for one and took a big bite. The lime juice tingled her taste buds while the mashed avocado cooled it off. "It's delicious."

"This is my favorite." The man handed her a skewer of petite shrimp. "It's smoked shrimp with freshly squeezed lemon juice, fresh basil and garlic, smoked in Applewood chips."

Millie popped the tasty morsels in her mouth. "This is hands down one of the best shrimp I've ever tasted."

"There's one more. Parmesan tuiles topped with chopped tomatoes tossed in olive oil and herbs."

"Thank you." She gobbled up her goodies and dabbed at her mouth with the cocktail napkin. "Now, I can skip dinner."

Another server appeared offering a tray of champagne. Millie smiled politely and shook her head.

A second one passed by with sparkling water. Millie grabbed two flutes and waited for Nic, who was wrapping up his speech.

He caught Millie's eye and started to make his way over when a female passenger intercepted him.

He gave Millie a small shrug and escorted the woman onto the dance floor where a three-piece orchestra had begun playing.

There was a light tap on her shoulder, and Millie turned to find Thomas Windsor standing directly behind her. "Millie Armati."

"Mr. Windsor."

"Thomas. Please call me Thomas."

"Thomas. Are you enjoying your cruise?"

"Immensely." His eyes slowly scanned the crowded lounge. "You know how to host an event. The drinks and appetizers are a nice touch."

"This was all Andy Walker's idea." Millie offered Thomas one of the glasses of sparkling water.

"Thank you." Windsor took a sip, eyeing Millie over the rim. "It's been a wonderful voyage so far. I love the sea days, walking up on deck early in the morning, the cool ocean breeze in my hair."

His expression sobered. "I heard about the poor entertainer's tragic death on our first night at sea. Rumor has it she was pushed over the side, but some are saying she went over on her own."

"I...we're not sure what happened yet." Millie didn't want to lie, but she also didn't want to start a rumor over the cause of Wendy's death. "It's a tragic situation."

"Would you..." Before Windsor could finish his sentence, a petite woman with meticulously coiffed hair and dripping with diamonds, timidly tapped him on the shoulder. "Hello, Thomas."

"Isabelle." Thomas moved to the side so the woman could join them.

"I'm sorry to bother you, but wondered if I might take you up on your offer to sweep me off my feet and around the dance floor."

Millie could see he was torn between abandoning her and accepting the offer. She reached for his half-empty glass. "I don't mean to hog Mr. Windsor - Thomas. Please...go on ahead."

Windsor gave Millie a grateful smile before taking the woman's arm and escorting her onto the dance floor.

A sudden movement near the stage caught Millie's attention. A group of women stood watching Thomas and Isabelle, a look of anger on their faces as the couple began circling the floor. One in particular shot daggers at them, a thunderous expression on her face as Thomas leaned in to whisper something in Isabelle's ear.

Determined to head off a confrontation, Millie made her way along the edge of the dance floor and toward the group of women. But it was too late.

A dark-haired woman, the one with the murderous look, grabbed Isabelle's arm and yanked her out of Thomas's arms.

Isabelle's look of adoration vanished, quickly replaced by one that rivaled the other woman's expression. She shoved the woman, and the two began screaming at each other.

Thomas attempted to smooth things over, which only infuriated the other woman.

"Womanizer!" Enraged, she took a swing at him, aiming for his face.

To his credit, Thomas was fast. He managed to duck, but not fast enough to escape the woman's wrath. Her clenched fist grazed the top of Thomas's head.

The "Silver Fox's" shiny locks lifted off and became airborne, the tips glowing in the soft lights as they sailed effortlessly, like a cloud with a silver lining sailing through the air until they landed on the floor directly in front of a speaker.

Millie had reached the scene by then. Both she and Windsor dove for the lost locks, colliding head-on and landing in a heap on the floor.

The disco ball gleamed brightly on Thomas's smooth, shiny scalp. He quickly snatched up his hairpiece and attempted to place it back atop his head.

"I'm so sorry," Millie gasped. "Here...let me help." She adjusted the man's toupee until it looked straight.

Nic rushed over to help his wife and Thomas to their feet. "Are you two okay?"

"Yes. It was just a minor collision." Millie swiped at her pants, turning her attention to the troublemakers, who stood off to the side looking slightly chagrined. "What is going on? You attacked poor Thomas and Isabelle."

The dark-haired woman shot her a defiant look and glared at Thomas. "This man is a player. He promised us a dance, and then he flaunts old Izzy here right in front of our faces without checking his dance card first. I'm not going to put up with it."

The woman straightened her shoulders and with one more sizzling glare in Thomas's direction, stomped off the stage. The other women hurried after her, leaving only Thomas, Isabelle, Nic and Millie.

"I'm sorry, Thomas," Isabelle apologized. "I didn't mean to cause you any trouble. Are you okay?"

"I'm fine." He picked at a piece of lint on his jacket. "Just suffering from a little wounded pride. I guess I know who to take off my dance card." He turned to Millie. "Thanks for the backup."

"You're welcome. I'm sorry the women caused a scene."

"All's well that ends well." Thomas crooked his elbow. "Shall we resume our dance?"

"We shall." Isabelle's dazzling smile returned as she took Thomas's arm and they stepped back onto the dance floor.

Millie turned to her husband. "The ladies appear to be swooning over the captain, as well."

"And I only have eyes for one woman." Nic grasped Millie's hand and they circled the floor. Her pulse ticked up a notch when the music slowed and he pulled her closer.

A shiver ran down her spine, and she tightened her grip. "Keep that up, and we'll have to call in sick for the rest of our shift," she teased.

"And that's a bad thing?" Nic whispered. "Don't tempt me."

The song ended, and they reluctantly exited the floor. "I must get back to the bridge."

Millie followed her husband to the door. "We'll continue our romantic evening and dance when we get home."

"You must've read my mind." Nic's eyes smoldered. "Promise?"

Millie lowered her eyelids. "Absolutely."

He gave his wife a quick kiss and then turned on his heel, a spring in his step as he sauntered out of sight.

Millie consulted her scheduler. It was almost time for Blackjack and Danielle to begin the first of their two evening shows.

There was no way she would have time to wrap up the Mix and Mingles and make it to the show if she stopped by the gift shop. The quickest way for Millie to obtain information on the two crewmembers was to send a text to Cat's cell phone.

She tapped out a message, giving her friend both men's names and asking her to look them up before returning to the party.

Thomas Windsor was among the last to leave. He reached for Millie's hand and gallantly placed a light kiss on the top. "Thanks again for the backup."

"You're most welcome. You sure know how to liven up a party," she teased. "I'm surprised you haven't proposed marriage to one of these lovely women yet."

"No more marriages for me," Thomas said. "I do enjoy the company. I already have my dance card filled for the next senior singles event."

"Minus the troublemakers," Millie joked. "I'm sure there will be more parties once Andy discovers how popular this one was."

"I would call this a resounding success. I do apologize for the small scene earlier. I have an uncanny ability to bring out the best...and worst in the women." Thomas quickly changed the subject. "If I may make a suggestion, I would move it to a larger venue."

"I agree. It was a little...shall we say...cozy."

"Cozy. That's an appropriate description." Windsor motioned to the door. "I see my dinner date waiting in the hallway. I must be going."

Millie stayed near the exit waiting for the last of the stragglers, all of whom thanked her for hosting the event and inquiring about the next one.

Her cell phone chimed while she was chatting with a passenger. She waited until she was alone to check it. Cat had sent her a text message.

Millie double clicked on the message, and her breath caught in her throat as she read the text.

Chapter 17

"Hey, Millie. Sorry it took so long to get back with you. I researched the two employees you sent me. Bartrand Melbane was issued his ship's identification in September of 2016. He transferred from the crew kitchen back in January and now works in room service. Justin Fleming has been employed by Majestic Cruise Lines since 2018. He works in the pizza station and the deli. I hope this helps."

Millie texted a reply. "Are there employee photo IDs?"

"Yes, but they're kind of blurry. You can swing by to have a look."

Millie's heart sank as she consulted her watch. As much as she wanted to delve into the identity of the two men, she would have to put her sleuthing on the backburner.

*****

The theater was packed and not an empty seat left for the early show.

Millie wondered how Danielle was holding up and if she knew how many people would be watching. She climbed the side stairs to the theater's second level and found an empty spot in the corner not far from the door.

Music began to play as the curtains opened, and Andy stepped onto the stage. Millie half-listened as she mulled over Cat's information. Both men worked in food service, which wasn't surprising. Half of the jobs on board the ship were either food related or in beverage service.

Annette claimed she didn't recognize the man in the photo, so perhaps he worked a different shift for one of the other kitchen supervisors.

If Millie wanted to track them down, she would need to get creative. She turned her cell phone on and studied the picture of Blackjack and the mystery crewmember. She would give anything to have been close enough to overhear the conversation between the men.

The show began, and Millie turned her attention to Blackjack and Danielle. She watched the fish tank and fish bowl magic trick again, and still had no idea how the man was able to turn water into coins and then coins into goldfish.

Millie slipped out of the theater moments later. It was time to give Sharky the good news.

She reached the maintenance office where she found Reef inside and behind the desk. "Is Sharky around?"

"He's gone for the day."

Millie averted her gaze, forcing herself to look away from Reef's unusual eye patch tattoo. "I promised to get back with him before the end of the day."

"You can probably catch him up in the employee computer area. He likes to hang out there after he's done working."

"To chat with his girlfriend?" Millie's hand flew to her mouth. "I didn't mean to say that."

Reef waved dismissively. "You're not telling me anything I don't already know. He's got it bad for Svetlana. I tried to warn him about these Russian mail order brides, but he's convinced that he's finally met his one true love."

Millie's eyes grew wide. "Russian mail order bride?"

"You didn't hear it from me. He's been wiring her money so she can meet him in Southampton."

"I don't think that's a good idea."

"Me, either, but you know Sharky. Once he gets something stuck in his head, he won't give it up."

Millie knew exactly what Reef meant. It had taken him a long time to get over his infatuation with Annette. In fact, Sharky seemed to enjoy the chase, convinced she would eventually succumb to his irresistible charm. "I'll try to track him down."

"Remember, you didn't hear about the mail order thing from me," Reef said.

"My lips are sealed." Millie made a zipping motion across her lips. "I'll see if I can talk some sense into him while I'm at it."

"Good luck."

Millie thanked him for the heads up and then climbed the stairs to deck one. Reef was right. Sharky was in the computer room. There was another employee in the room but on the opposite end.

She squeezed along the narrow walkway and approached Sharky, his expression intense, and his eyes fixed on the computer screen.

Finally, he looked up. "Lookie here. It's Millie Armati. I thought you pooped out on your end of our bargain."

"Nope." Millie pulled out a chair. "I talked to Cat. She isn't going to write off the beef jerky, but said if you stop by the store tomorrow, she'll give you an employee purchase order and you can make payments."

"Payments?" Sharky growled. "The jerky is long gone."

"It's your only option. Take it or leave it."

He frowned. "Fine. It's better than nothing. What about the other...the time off in Southampton?"

"I'm worried about you, Sharky, going off and meeting strange women in a foreign country."

"Shhh." Sharky glanced over Millie's shoulder and pressed a finger to his lips. "You don't have to announce it to the world. Besides, it's none of your business."

"You're right. It isn't any of my business, but I'm still concerned. How well do you know Svetlana?"

"Well enough to know we're a match made in heaven."

Millie interrupted. 'You said the same thing about Annette."

"Annette who?"

"Annette, the love of your life, Delacroix."

"I was kidding. Of course, I remember Annette. I'm finally over her constant rejection. I'm ready for a little romance, and Svetlana fits the bill."

Millie wrinkled her nose. "Do you even know what she looks like?"

"Of course." Sharky shifted his chair to the side and motioned for Millie to join him. "I got a picture of her right here."

Millie slid closer and studied the woman's profile picture. The buxom blonde was leaning against a towering tree, one hand on her hip.

Her long flowing locks cascaded over her shoulders, the ends resting on the top of her low-cut blouse. She was smiling...and young. "How old is she?"

"Thirty-seven, going on twenty-something." He jabbed Millie with his elbow. "She's a real looker, huh?"

"She's very attractive. Are you sure this is the woman you've been communicating with?"

"One hundred percent. This one is the real deal, a keeper for sure." Sharky grinned from ear-to-ear. "She's got one sexy voice to match her sizzlin' good looks." He tapped the mouse, and a gravelly voice began speaking.

"Ve vill meet at za Blue Star Tavern Friday, May twenty-fifth at noon. If it is agreeable, we can discuss getting a room."

Sharky jabbed the keyboard to stop the recording. "The conversation gets a little racy after that, but you get the picture."

"Yes. Yes. I do." Millie stared at the woman. "You still don't know her." She turned to face him. "You're not giving her money, are you?"

"Me?" Sharky lifted a brow innocently. "Why would I give her money?"

"So she can fly to Southampton to meet you."

"I didn't give her money."

The way Sharky answered made Millie suspicious. "Did you *loan* her money?"

"Maybe." Sharky quickly turned the monitor and Millie guessed there was something else he didn't want her to see.

"This is a terrible idea. What if she's playing you?"

"Nobody plays Sharky Kiveski." He jabbed a finger at his chest. "I'm the one who does the playing, not the other way around. Like I said..."

"I know. It's none of my business." Millie sucked in a breath as she reached into her front pocket and pulled out the time off sheet Donovan had given her. "Against my better judgment, I'm giving you this. It's Donovan's approval for time off the day we reach Southampton."

"Sweet." Sharky snatched the sheet from Millie's hand and eyed it closely. He pressed it to his lips, smacking loudly. "You're the best. You made me the happiest man on board the ship."

"You're welcome, I think." Millie reluctantly stood. "I still get a bad feeling about this."

She could see Sharky was only half-listening. "Svetlana is back online."

"I'll let you get back to her."

Sharky didn't acknowledge Millie's departure, his eyes glued to the computer screen. She cast a wary glance in his direction and made a mental note to chat with him again when they got closer to Southampton.

Millie swung by Ocean Treasures, but the store was busy, and it was time for her to get back to work. She made her rounds, from the top of the ship to the lido deck, moving forward to aft as she checked on the various evening activities.

The lido deck party was in full swing, and she caught a glimpse of Thomas Windsor cutting the rug. He noticed Millie as she passed by and winked at her as he twirled one of the ladies in a jitterbug move.

Millie continued down the stairs, past the evening art auction, the first round of karaoke and then back upstairs to the gift shop.

Cat was hosting the "Bermuda Blowout" sale. The place was elbow-to-elbow with large clusters of people gathered around the $4.99 bargain priced t-shirt tables.

She kept going until she reached the galley. Annette was nowhere in sight, but Amit was there, his back to the door.

Millie cleared her throat as she approached the counter.

Amit turned. "Miss Millie. You are here late."

"I was hoping Annette was around."

"She's in a staff meeting. Is there something I can do for you?"

"As a matter of fact." Millie turned her cell phone on and showed Amit the picture of Blackjack and the mysterious Siren of the Seas' employee. "Do you recognize the man in the ball cap?"

"I don't think so, but it's hard to tell since he's not in uniform, and they are far away."

"That's what Annette said, too. Do the names Bartrand Melbane or Justin Fleming ring a bell? One of them works in room service and the other in the pizza and deli area."

"No." Amit shrugged helplessly. "There are many employees on board the ship. I hardly ever leave the kitchen unless it's helping out with room service orders or checking on the food."

"I think one of them may have been Wendy's boyfriend, Jerry Dean. I need to track them down."

"You could eat pizza, order deli sandwiches and room service to see if one of them shows up," Amit suggested.

"Actually food sounds good." The appetizers from the singles party were long gone. "Maybe I'll swing by the deli and grab a bite to eat."

She thanked Amit and headed upstairs to the buffet area where the kitchen staff was preparing the late night chocolate extravaganza. Millie circled the stations, admiring the chefs' creations.

"Hey." Annette, who was on the other side of the buffet, gave Millie a wave and made her way over.

"I thought you were in a meeting."

"I was." Annette pointed to a group of kitchen staff members who were standing next to a chocolate fountain, surrounded by platters of fresh fruit. "We were going over some changes to the chocolate buffet. What's up?"

"I'm here to grab a quick bite to eat."

"I'll join you. Amit is holding down the fort."

"I know. I just left the galley."

The women made their way to the grill station, each ordering a burger before carrying their food to a corner table. While they ate, Millie filled Annette in on what she'd found out about the two male crewmembers who boarded the ship right before she did. "They both work in food service."

"Since the men work nights, they report to the night supervisor, and I would have little contact with them," Annette said.

"I figured that might be the case." Millie took a big bite of burger and began chewing thoughtfully. "Cat told me there are photo IDs, but the pictures are blurry. I stopped by the gift shop to check them out. The place was packed."

"Cat's holding one of her blowout sales." Annette munched on a pickle spear. "How was Danielle's performance?"

"It was great." Millie told her friend she needed to catch the act. "You better not wait too long. Danielle isn't keen on this whole front-of-the-stage gig."

"I don't blame her." Annette downed the rest of her burger and soda. "I better get back to work."

"I'm right behind you." Millie finished the rest of her iced tea.

"Hold up." Annette nodded to someone standing in the doorway. "You're never gonna guess who just walked in."

Chapter 18

"Andy?" Millie started to turn.

"It's Dave Patterson, and he's looking our way."

Patterson strode purposefully across the room. He gave Annette a curt nod before addressing Millie. "Blackjack Blaze just left my office."

"Was he able to give you any leads on Wendy's alleged boyfriend?"

"No. He told me you followed him off the ship in Bermuda and are accusing him of being involved in Wendy's death."

"What?" Millie squeaked. "I never accused him of anything."

"Did you follow him off the ship?"

"I did *not*. Andy gave me a couple of hours off. Cat and I did a little shopping at the port stores and then returned to the ship."

"And did you see Blackjack during your time on shore?"

"I saw him talking to another crewmember not far from the dock. Cat and I both saw him. When I returned to the ship, I mentioned it to him. He claims the only people he met with were Wendy's family." Millie removed her cell phone from her pocket and scrolled to the picture of Blackjack and the unidentified crewmember.

"As you can clearly see, this is Blackjack and another man. I watched the man in the ball cap - a Siren of the Seas' employee - pass through the security checkpoint."

"This is certainly Blackjack. Forward me a copy." He handed the phone back. "You don't know who the other man is?"

"No, although I think I have it narrowed down," Millie said. "His name is either Bartrand Melbane or Justin Fleming. They both boarded the ship around the same time as the man in the picture."

"You're sure?"

"No. It's an educated guess...based on some information I obtained. Melbane works in room service delivery, and Fleming works in the deli/pizza area."

Patterson turned to Annette. "I'm going to take a wild guess that Millie already showed this photo to you. Do you recognize the man?"

Annette shook her head. "It's hard to tell from a distance, and the guy is wearing street clothes. I don't recognize either of those names. He could be a night shifter."

Patterson removed a notepad and pen from his pocket. "I'll look into it." He finished scribbling and addressed Millie. "Why would Blackjack accuse you of following him?"

"I have no idea," Millie shrugged. "Unless he's ticked I caught him talking to a crewmember off the ship and is trying to hide something."

"I suppose it's possible." Patterson nodded absentmindedly. "He was insistent you were following him."

"He can insist all he wants. Cat can back up the facts."

"I'll chat with Cat, as well." Patterson motioned to Millie's cell phone. "Don't forget to send me the picture."

"I will."

Patterson walked away, and Millie waited until he was gone. "Why would Blackjack claim I followed him off the ship...unless he has something to hide? Something doesn't smell right."

"Danielle's been spending a lot of time with him going over their routine. Why don't you ask her if she's noticed any unusual behavior?"

"That's a great idea." Millie followed Annette to the sliding doors and stepped onto the open deck.

"In the meantime, I'll keep my eyes and ears open and let you know if I find anything out about Melbane or Fleming," Annette promised.

After she left, Millie sent Danielle a quick text, but she never replied.

Late night Killer Karaoke was Millie's next event. The event ended, and she headed to the comedy show where it was standing room only.

Millie kept moving, stopping only when Danielle finally replied. *I'm in the dressing room. What's up?*

Stay there. I'm on my way. Millie hurried down the steps, through the now empty theater and to the back of the stage where she found Felix and Danielle.

"You missed Danielle's superb performances," Felix gushed. "She's a natural."

Danielle began smoothing her hair into her signature ponytail. "It was horrible. Alison caked a thick layer of makeup on my face. It'll take a putty knife to scrape the gunk off. To top it all off, my feet are killing me."

"So you had fun," Millie joked.

Danielle shot her a dark look.

"Kidding. I was kidding. I caught the beginning of one of the performances and it was great."

"You were smashing, darling. Enjoy the limelight. It's *the* best part of show biz. I'll see you tomorrow." Felix gave Danielle an air kiss on each side of her cheek and then sashayed out of the dressing room, leaving the women alone.

"You have any luck figuring out who Blackjack met with in port today?"

"No. You'll never guess what he said about me." Millie briefly told her friend about Patterson's visit to the buffet, how Blackjack claimed she was following him.

"He thinks you're stalking him?" Danielle asked. "That's crazy."

"My guess is he's freaked out because I caught him talking to a crewmember. I wonder what he would think if he knew I had a picture of him and the mystery man? Which reminds me..." Millie sent Patterson a copy of the picture she'd snapped earlier. "He's hiding something."

Danielle finished rubbing off the gobs of makeup and tossed the tissues in the trash. "Despite his entertainer status, he strikes me as a very private person. He also seemed like he was in a big hurry to get out of here tonight - like he had somewhere he needed to be."

"Another meeting with the mystery man," Millie mused.

"Maybe. After the second show, he asked me if I would meet him for another practice first thing tomorrow morning. Then, he got some sort of message on his phone and changed it to nine o'clock."

"So something pressing came up?"

"Could be," Danielle shrugged. "He seemed very distracted and in a hurry to take off."

"What time were you originally scheduled to meet him?"

"Seven-thirty."

Millie pressed her palms together. "So he has something going on first thing tomorrow morning...something important."

"That would be my guess."

"Let me check my schedule." Millie consulted her scheduler. "Crud. I'm hosting a seven-thirty Sunrise Stretch."

"Find someone who'll swap with you," Danielle studied her scheduler. "I have a six a.m. daybreak donut event, but coffee consumption and donut devouring should only take about an hour."

"Who could I get to swap?"

"Try asking Tara. She loves those early morning classes."

"Good idea." Millie radioed Tara who was happy to swap Millie's Sunrise Stretch in exchange for her hosting a beginner macramé class.

"Thanks, Tara. I owe you one." Millie clipped her radio to her belt and gave Danielle a thumbs up. "We'll meet tomorrow morning at seven-thirty outside your cabin and see if we can figure out what Blackjack is up to."

"What if he doesn't do anything?" Danielle asked. "Maybe he just doesn't like getting up early."

"It's possible, although you said he seemed distracted, which leads me to believe there's a reason he changed his schedule."

"And you think it has to do with Wendy's death?"

"I don't know. What I do know is that I have to be careful. Patterson will be breathing down my neck if he suspects we're spying on Blackjack."

"We have legitimate reasons to be in the crew area," Danielle pointed out. "Blackjack can fuss all he wants. Unless he can prove it, there's nothing he - or Patterson - can do."

"True. It's just..." Millie absentmindedly patted her pocket. Following Blackjack was a risk she would have to take. "Never mind. It's not like I haven't been in trouble a time or two."

"Or a half dozen." Danielle slid out of the seat and limped toward the exit.

"Did you hurt yourself?" Millie cast her friend a look of concern.

"The high heels I wore during the show are a killer. It was a struggle to stay vertical and not fall flat on my face."

"I know you hate this whole showbiz deal, but I'm with Felix on this one. You wowed the crowd." Millie patted her friend's arm. "You're a natural."

"I'm a natural all right. A natural klutz. Mark my words…before this gig ends, I'm gonna hit the floor and probably break a limb."

"Nah," Millie waved dismissively. "You got this. Besides, the more you practice the better you'll get."

The women parted ways in the stairwell. Millie headed toward the gift shop before realizing it had already closed. Hoping Cat might still be inside, she slowed when she reached the entrance, but the store was empty.

With nothing left to do and her shift ending, it was time to go home.

Nic was on the bridge with another of the staff captains. He motioned for her to wait and then accompanied her to their apartment door. "I was beginning to wonder if you were coming home."

"I got sidetracked." Millie reached for her keycard, and Nic dashed in front of her. "Wait…I have a surprise."

Chapter 19

Nic opened the apartment door, grabbed her hand and didn't let go until they reached the living room. He strode to the other side to a portable CD player sitting on the coffee table. "I didn't forget about our dance earlier."

He returned to Millie's side as soft music began to play. "May I have this dance, my beautiful bride?"

Millie's heart skipped a beat as their eyes met. "Of course." She let Nic lead her to the center of the living room. She stepped into his arms, and they began to sway. Around and around they went.

She closed her eyes, thanking God for giving her such a wonderful husband. She blinked back the sudden tears. If she left the earth today, she would die a happy woman. Millie Armati had lived a fairytale life with her Prince Charming.

They danced for several songs before the music ended.

"Stay here." Nic stepped into the kitchen and returned carrying a stunning bouquet of long-stemmed red roses.

"Nic." Millie's breath caught in her throat. "They're beautiful."

"Not nearly as beautiful as you."

She cautiously took the bouquet, slowly turning it as she admired the roses. "Thank you. I...you're so sweet. I don't know what I ever did to deserve you, but I thank God every day I'm your wife."

She set the bouquet on the end table and placed her hands on both sides of her husband's face. "You've given me a perfect ending to a hectic day. There aren't enough words to tell you how much I love you with all my heart."

"I love you, too, Millie Armati, and I will for the rest of my life."

*****

Millie was up early the next morning. She woke before Nic and slipped into the bathroom to get ready. By the time she returned, their bed was made and the bedroom empty.

She reached the bottom of the stairs and the smell of freshly brewed coffee wafted into the living room. Nic was sitting in front of the computer.

"Thanks for the coffee." Millie poured a cup and joined him. "Whatcha' doing?"

"I'm reading an email from Fiona. She's asking about our summer schedule."

"Oh?" Millie cautiously sipped her coffee. Fiona, Nic's only child, did not care for his father's new wife. In fact, during their honeymoon in St. Martin, she caused a scene in the restaurant, made some unflattering comments aimed at Millie and stormed out.

Nic had attempted to smooth things over but it was glaringly apparent Fiona did not care for her. She left the island the next morning, and they hadn't seen her since.

Millie had hoped that with time Fiona would come around. "Does she plan to join us on board the ship?"

"She hasn't decided yet. If not, I thought we could head home to visit her and also visit some of my old stomping grounds."

"I would love to. Perhaps this time Fiona won't be so...verbal about her dislike for me."

Nic reached for his wife's hand. "I'm sorry she hurt your feelings and caused a scene. It was hard on Fiona, after Lisa's death. I think once she gets to know you, you two will hit it off."

Millie had her doubts but knew it was important to Nic that she and his daughter attempt to develop some sort of relationship or at the very least a tolerance for one another. She had prayed about it, decided to leave it in God's hands and let him lead the way.

"I've been praying about it." Millie forced a smile. "I should get going."

She finished the last of her coffee and rinsed the cup in the sink. "I'm hoping for a stress-free day. I'm off to a good start. Andy hasn't sent me any new schedule changes."

She slipped her shoes on and reached for her lanyard that was hanging on the hook by the door.

Nic joined her. "Do you think you could ask Annette for another starter of her delicious bread?"

"I already did. She promised she would give me another one just as soon as it's ready." Millie bounced on her tiptoes and kissed her husband good-bye.

She reached Danielle's cabin at seven-fifteen on the dot, and gave the door a light tap.

The door flew open. "You're early." Danielle wiggled into her work shoes, and joined Millie in the hall. The women picked up the pace as they made their way to the other end of the crews' quarters.

They passed Blackjack's cabin, walked to the other end of the hall and rounded the corner, stopping as soon as they were out of sight.

"We can't just stand here. Blackjack is already complaining I'm spying on him." Millie tapped her foot impatiently. "What about hanging out in the crew mess hall?"

"He might go there. It's as good a place as any to start." Danielle took a step and stopped at the sound of rattling coming from the hall they'd just passed through.

A crewmember emerged from one of the cabins and began walking toward them.

Millie casually leaned a hip against the wall as the woman passed by. She shot Danielle and Millie a puzzled look but never slowed.

Thud. A dull thud echoed from the corridor. Danielle pressed a finger to her lips, craning her neck. It was Blackjack. He exited his cabin and headed in the opposite direction before disappearing from sight.

Danielle grabbed Millie's hand, and they began following him, careful to stay far enough back and not draw attention to themselves.

Blackjack slowed when he reached the crew dining room. Millie thought he was going inside, but instead he disappeared into the stairwell on the opposite side of the hall.

The women hurried to the exit. Millie reached for the door handle and counted to five before opening it. She eased forward and slowly lifted her gaze. She could make out the soles of Blackjack's shoes as he clomped up the stairs.

He exited onto deck three, not far from the entrance to the theater's lower level.

"Let's go." Millie raced up the stairs, taking them two at a time. She reached deck three and waited for Danielle to catch up.

"You got jet packs on those shoes?" she gasped.

"Nope. Just plenty of practice taking the stairs." Millie pushed the door open, and the women stepped into the empty lobby. "We lost him."

"He may be on his way to Andy's office."

"Could be." Millie hurried to the other side of the ship and the main corridor. It was empty, too. Blackjack appeared to have vanished into thin air. "He didn't go that way."

"Blackjack can't accuse you of following him to your boss's office," Danielle said.

"You're right." The women entered the dark theater. It took Millie's eyes a second to adjust to the lack of light before they strolled down the center aisle.

Andy's office was empty. The women checked the dressing area next, but there wasn't a soul in sight.

"This was a bust. I'm sorry you changed your morning schedule for nothing," Danielle said.

"Don't apologize. It was partly my idea. Besides, it was worth a shot." Millie led the way as they retraced their steps and exited the theater.

She let Danielle go ahead as she slowed to consult her scheduler. Millie wasn't watching where she was going and collided with her friend, clipping the back of Danielle's shoe. "Whoops."

She realized there was a reason for her friend's sudden stop. Blackjack and another man stood near the bank of elevators, talking in low voices.

"Hey, Blackjack," Danielle called out.

Blackjack's back stiffened, and he slowly turned to face them. "Danielle. Millie. You're up early."

"We're always up early." Millie turned her attention to the other man. "Hello."

The man offered her a faint smile.

"Speaking of early," Blackjack said. "I have a busy day and need to get going."

Millie ignored him as she extended her hand to the man. "I'm Millie Armati, Assistant Cruise Director."

He stared at her hand for a moment before reluctantly shaking it. "Justin Fleming."

"Justin Fleming." Millie's heart skipped a beat as she glanced at his work uniform. "You work on board the ship."

"I do."

"In food service?" Millie persisted.

"Uh...yeah. I work at the pizza station."

Blackjack eased past Justin, and Fleming reached out to stop him. "Hang on. We still have a small matter to discuss."

"Not now. I'm late for a breakfast meeting with the cruise director." He turned on his heel and strode out of the corridor.

Millie was determined that Fleming wouldn't escape quite as easily and turned to Danielle. "This is Danielle Kneldon. She works in the entertainment department, as well."

"Nice to meet you." Justin smiled at Danielle.

"I'm a regular at the pizza place," Millie said. "I've never seen you around."

"I work the graveyard shift. In fact, I just got off work."

"I see." Millie motioned in the direction of where Blackjack had departed. "You know Blackjack?"

"I do." He shifted his feet.

Millie lifted her chin. Now was her chance to catch Fleming off guard. "I figured you must be friends. In fact, I saw you two in Bermuda the other day not far from the port. I was going to stop by to say hello to Blackjack, but you were in the middle of a serious conversation."

Justin nervously cleared his throat. "Yes. We...uh...bumped into each other."

"Did you meet Blackjack while working on another cruise ship?" Millie could see the young man was growing increasingly uncomfortable with her questions.

"We met through a mutual friend." Justin turned to go.

Millie reached out to stop him. "You met through Wendy."

Justin's eyes grew wide. "No. I mean. I knew Blackjack before I met Wendy. We hung out at the same bars in Miami."

"Have you talked to Dave Patterson, the head of security, about Wendy's death?" Millie asked softly. "You should tell him you knew her."

The color drained from Justin's face. "You can't. I mean. I didn't hurt Wendy. I didn't even know she was on the ship."

"You didn't see Wendy after she boarded on Saturday?"

"No." Justin took a quick step back. "She never found me."

"Because you lied to her about your identity. You told her your name was Jerry Dean, not Justin Fleming." Millie figured she was on the right track based on the man's reaction. "Why did you lie to Wendy about who you were?"

"It was a fling. I had no idea she would hunt me down. This is Blackjack's fault. We had a deal. He was supposed to keep his mouth shut."

"Why?" Danielle, who had so far remained silent, spoke. "Why was Blackjack supposed to keep quiet?"

"We had a deal," he repeated as he began backing away. "I had nothing to do with Wendy's death."

269

"You need to talk to Dave Patterson, to tell him who you are," Millie said. "If you want to help, to find out what happened to Wendy, you need to come clean."

"Then Patterson needs to take a closer look at Blackjack," Justin blurted out.

"I agree," Millie said. "But in the meantime..."

Justin's distressed look quickly became defiant. "What if I don't? I haven't committed a crime."

"Then I'll tell him," Millie warned. "If you have nothing to hide, it will look much better for you if you approach him rather than Patterson having to track you down."

Justin clenched his fist. "This is none of your business."

"A close friend of mine, an innocent man, is being investigated." Millie crossed her arms. "I'll let you decide. Are you going to go to Patterson, or am I?"

The muscle in his jaw twitched as he glared at Millie. "I'll go."

"Now," Millie said.

The man made a grunting noise before stomping off. He yanked the crew exit door open and stepped inside. The door slammed behind him.

"That went well," Danielle joked.

"As well as can be expected," Millie sighed. "At least we have a positive ID on the mystery man Blackjack met in Bermuda. He might as well have admitted he was the father of Wendy's baby."

"You think he killed her?" Danielle asked.

"I'm leaning in that direction." Millie pondered the new information. "Except for the fact Blackjack has been meeting with Justin since Wendy's death. Why didn't Blackjack tell Patterson about him? Justin said something about Blackjack keeping his mouth shut. There's more going on here than meets the eye."

"Patterson will get to the bottom of it." Millie's scheduler chimed and seconds later, so did Danielle's.

"We're being summoned." Millie glanced at the screen. "A 911 meeting in Andy's office. I have a funny feeling this involves Blackjack."

The women returned to the theater, to the back and Andy's office. He was inside and alone. "That was fast."

"We were standing in the hallway." Millie pulled out a chair. "What's up?"

"Blackjack just left. We briefly discussed Danielle's performance last night, and he asked me to find a replacement."

"He thinks I did a crappy job?"

"Those weren't his exact words." Andy leaned his elbows on the desk. "He said he thought someone else might be better suited for the job."

"Fine with me." Danielle tossed her scheduler on the conference table. "That's the best news I've heard since we left port. Maybe Isla can take my place."

"I'm already working on it." Andy turned to Millie. "Blackjack told me he thinks you're following him around the ship, spying on him."

"That's crazy," Millie said. "He told Patterson the same thing."

"You accused him of meeting someone in Bermuda who didn't exist..."

"Justin Fleming," Millie interrupted.

"Who is Justin Fleming?"

"The imaginary man. Danielle and I just ran into him and Blackjack in the hall. I believe Fleming is the father of Wendy's baby, and for some reason, Blackjack has been keeping it quiet."

Andy stared at Millie in disbelief. "Why hasn't Blackjack turned Fleming in to Patterson?"

"That's an excellent question. Maybe he's holding something over Blackjack's head...a reason he's keeping quiet."

Andy pushed his chair back, and it hit the floor with a loud thud.

"Fleming is on his way to Patterson's office. I told him he needed to go of his own free will, or I would report him."

"I don't know how you manage to get right in the middle of these messes." Andy shook his head.

"Sometimes even I'm surprised," Millie said.

"The investigation and ship security is Patterson's problem." Andy jabbed his finger at Danielle. "In the meantime, you're off the hook for the shows."

"Sweet." Danielle beamed as she sprang from her chair. "I couldn't be happier."

"And you..."Andy turned to Millie. "Stay away from Blackjack."

"I will." Millie slowly stood. "He's safe from me stalking him, unless he plans on participating in a beginner's macramé class."

"Very funny."

Danielle followed Millie out of Andy's office. "What do you think?"

"Blackjack is keeping a secret, and I intend to find out what it is."

"You heard Andy. He told you to steer clear of Blackjack."

"I will," Millie said. "But I didn't promise not to try to figure out why Blackjack denied knowing Justin and why he didn't turn him in to Patterson."

Chapter 20

Millie was all thumbs during the macramé class. With some extra assistance from the instructor who helped her finish the ends, she triumphantly waved her creation in the air. "Ta-da."

"You did it, Millie. Good job."

"You think so?" She inspected her beaded, burnt orange bookmark. "It looks kinda messy."

"It's an excellent first attempt. There's always next time."

"We'll have to see about that." Millie helped the woman pack up her bins of materials and load them onto a rolling cart.

It was time for Millie to host a goofy golf contest on the sports deck. To add challenges to the game, she awarded participants extra points for odd shots.

After they finished, she passed out discount coupons to the specialty coffee shop.

Next up was trivia, followed by a quick break where Millie grabbed a bite to eat. She scooped some eggs onto her plate along with a small stack of paper-thin pancakes. She spied Isla, who was dining alone, and made her way to the table. "Mind if I join you?"

"Of course not." Isla slid her tray out of the way to make room. "How's your morning?"

"Busy." Millie eased her plate of food and cup of coffee onto the table. "I've already squeezed in a macramé class, putt putt golf and a round of trivia. How about you?"

Isla rattled off her list of morning events. "I got roped into assisting Blackjack, after all. We practiced for the upcoming performance. I'm not sure what happened. I thought Danielle did a great job last night."

"It was more of a personality conflict." Millie reached for a pat of butter. "What do you think of Blackjack?"

"He's okay, although he seemed a little on edge." Isla handed Millie the jar of syrup. "He kept asking questions about how mail was handled on board the ship."

"Mail as in postage stamp snail mail?"

"Yep." Isla nodded. "I told him he could receive mail in the ports via the company agent, but he was more interested in sending mail. He said he needed to mail a very important letter."

"Did you tell him that the mail is collected from a bin near guest services and is picked up when we're in port?" Millie asked. "I'm pretty sure it's given to the port agent to process."

"I did." Isla dipped her hash brown round in catsup and popped it into her mouth.

"I wonder what Blackjack needs to mail that's so important."

"I don't know. What I do know is he cut our practice short so he could take care of it. Not sure why he was in such a big hurry since we're not docking in the Azores for a couple more days."

Their conversation turned to activities on board the ship. Isla wolfed down the rest of her food and stood. "I better get going before Andy hunts me down."

After Isla left, Millie mulled over her comments about the outgoing mail. She polished off the last of her pancakes and headed to the bridge where she found Nic and several of the other officers gathered at the conference table.

She quietly made her way to the apartment where she let Scout out for a break. Millie left the sliders open, turned the computer on, and logged onto the ship's system.

Her hand hovered over the mouse as she seesawed back and forth over accessing Blaze's information. Deciding she could easily look him up online, she clicked on the ship's employee roster and typed in his name.

Blaze's legal name was Marvin Copper. It listed a Miami Gardens address. The picture of him was old, but she could tell it was an unsmiling Blackjack.

"Marvin Copper," Millie whispered. "What are you hiding?" She opened a new search screen and typed in Marvin Copper, Miami Gardens, Florida.

Several sites popped up, including Blackjack's professional website listing his credentials. She clicked on several results, but nothing hit her radar as suspicious.

Millie exited the search screens and logged off the computer before coaxing Scout back inside. With a few minutes to spare, she decided to swing by the galley to chat with Annette.

Her friend was in the kitchen, a bag of frosting in hand.

"Hey." Millie snuck up behind her and whispered in her ear.

Annette jumped, a small glob of frosting trailed across the counter. "You scared me half to death."

"Sorry. I only wanted to scare you a quarter to death," Millie joked. "What are you working on?"

"A cake for the specialty shop."

Millie swiped the frosting off the counter and licked her finger. "This is delicious. Speaking of delicious, Nic is still bugging me about your friendship bread starter."

"I can give you another one tomorrow." Annette turned her attention to the cake and began piping frosting along the edge. "I heard Blackjack kicked Danielle off his show."

"He did. He's also accusing me of spying on him. Danielle and I caught him talking with another crewmember first thing this morning. It was Justin Fleming, the same guy he denied meeting in Bermuda."

Millie laid out her theory that both Justin Fleming and Blackjack Blaze were hiding something. "Blackjack is keeping a secret for Fleming and Fleming is keeping a secret for Blackjack. Or maybe they're holding something over each other's head."

"A criminal record?" Annette dismissed the thought. "Nah. Both of them would've been screened before Majestic hired them. Maybe an unsavory lawsuit?"

"Could be," Millie said. "Isla is taking Danielle's place and practiced with him earlier today. She said Blackjack seemed very interested in the ship's snail mail service. Andy had booked Blackjack and his show last minute. Maybe he had some business he didn't have time to take care of before boarding the ship."

"We can go through the mail, to see if we can figure out what it is," Annette said. "The outgoing mail kiosk is next to the guest services desk."

"How are we going to pull that off?" An idea popped into Millie's head. "Wait a minute. I know someone who can go through the outgoing mail without it looking suspicious."

"Cat," Annette and Millie said in unison.

Millie warmed to the idea. "All she has to do is pretend she mailed something for Ocean Treasures and needs to get it back. It's brilliant." She thanked her friend for the idea and hurried out of the galley.

It was a short trip from the galley to the gift shop. Cat was inside with Lila, another of the store's employees. She gave her a quick wave and made a beeline for Cat. "You got a minute?"

"Sure. Are you here to take a look at the photos of the employees you asked me about?"

"Nope. I've already identified the man who was with Blackjack in Bermuda, but thanks for the offer," Millie said. "I need you to run down to the promenade deck, to the mail kiosk and sort through the outgoing mail. I think Blackjack mailed, or is going to mail, something important, and I want to know what it is."

"Isn't that against the law...to go through the mail?"

"We're not opening it...just sorting through it. You could pretend you dropped something in there for the store, and need to get it back out."

"But I didn't."

"You can do it right now." Millie darted to the postcard display. She skimmed through the selection and grabbed one with a picture of Siren of the Seas before returning to Cat's side. "Fill it out. I'll drop it in the box. Later today, we can run down there and retrieve it."

Cat pressed the back of her hand to Millie's forehead. "I think you're losing it."

Millie swatted her hand away. "I'm feeling fine. Please?"

"All right." Cat hesitantly reached for a pen. "Maybe Blackjack forgot to mail a bill or something." She finished filling it out and stuck a stamp in the corner.

Cat started to hand it to Millie before snatching it back. "When do you want to start digging...err...sifting through the mail?"

"What time do you get off work?"

"Ten-thirty tonight."

"I'll meet you here at ten-thirty. We'll go down together." Millie took the postcard from Cat and exited the store. She found the outgoing mailbox next to guest services and dropped the postcard inside.

The rest of the day passed by in a blur with a round of trivia, followed by bingo, and then she swung by to check on the art auction. Next up was a line dancing class before it was time for Millie to return home to get ready for the captain's dinner.

Nic was already in the apartment, changing out of his work uniform into his "event uniform" as Millie called it. He kept one suit crisp, clean and starched, specifically for public events.

"Look at you," Millie teased. "Two parties in two evenings."

"Andy has me all over the place." Nic snapped his cufflinks. "Are you able to join me for dinner this evening?"

"I am. Let me go change, and we'll head down to the pre-dinner festivities in the atrium." Millie flew up the stairs and swapped out her work uniform for a cocktail dress she'd purchased in Miami the previous week.

It was a beaded mesh short sleeve dress in a champagne color. She'd lucked out and found a pair of shoes the exact same shade. Millie fixed her hair and spritzed on some of her favorite perfume before returning downstairs.

Nic, who was waiting at the bottom of the steps, let out a low wolf whistle. "I love the new dress."

"Thanks." Millie's cheeks warmed. "I thought you might like it."

"I do." Nic placed a light hand on his wife's back and guided her out of the apartment.

The band had already set up and was beginning to play when the couple reached the atrium. Nic made his rounds while Millie mingled with the guests on the other side of the room.

Andy was on hand, as well as Donovan Sweeney, Staff Captain Vitale, Annette, who was in full chef's uniform, and several other officers.

The ship's photographer stuck close to Nic, who spent most of his time posing for pictures with the passengers. The pre-dinner festivities ended, and they headed to the dining room, where several diamond guests and Andy joined them.

Sanun, the captain's table waiter, hurried over. "Miss Millie, it's nice to see you." He handed her a menu.

"Thanks Sanun, my boss finally gave me some time off."

Andy shot her an irritated look. "I think I'm fairly flexible with staff schedules, whenever possible."

"You are. You're also an awesome boss, except when it comes to your experiments." She tapped the top of the scheduler.

"Give it time, Millie."

The server's assistant followed behind, filling the water goblets while Millie perused the dinner menu. When he returned, she placed her order and handed the menu to him.

The woman seated next to Millie complimented her on her dress.

"Thank you." Millie smoothed the front. "I just picked it up."

The woman leaned in. "You and the captain make a striking couple. How did you manage to snag the captain of a cruise ship?"

Nic, who had been placing his dinner order, turned to them. "My wife has a penchant for getting into trouble. She spent a lot of time in my office."

"I did not." Millie playfully punched her husband in the arm.

"Really?" Nic lifted a brow.

"Well. Maybe a couple of times."

The appetizers arrived, and while they ate, Nic and Andy bantered back and forth, entertaining the guests with stories of ship adventures.

Dinner ended, and Nic and Millie lingered over dessert and coffee, until Millie's scheduler chimed. "That's my reminder it's time to go."

Back at home, the couple swapped out their dress-up duds for work clothes and parted ways on the bridge.

Millie stopped long enough to catch a few minutes of the headliner show, Gem of the Seas, before checking on the lido deck events. Next up was a shuffleboard competition, followed by another round of karaoke.

Finally, it was time to meet Cat, who was already waiting for Millie in the corridor outside the gift shop. "Are you sure you want to do this?"

"Positive. We're looking for the name Marvin Copper, which is Blackjack's real name."

The guest services desk was down two decks and toward the center of the ship. Nikki Tan, Millie's friend who also happened to be her first cabin mate on board the ship, was working.

"Hey, Millie, Cat."

"Hi, Nikki," Millie greeted her. "You're not very busy tonight."

"Not now, but earlier this place was a madhouse." Nikki rolled her eyes. "If you're here to see Donovan, he's not in."

"We're not here to see Donovan." Cat stepped closer. "I dropped something in the mail kiosk earlier, and need to get it back out."

"Let me grab the keys." Nikki removed a set of keys from the desk drawer before making her way to the back of the mail bin and unlocking the cabinet.

Millie nudged Cat. "I can take over. I know what I'm looking for."

"Sure." Nikki shifted to the side to make room for Cat, and Millie joined her. "I'll help sort. Hand me a pile."

Cat reached inside and pulled out a handful of mail before passing it to Millie, who quickly thumbed through it.

A passenger made his way to the guest services line. "I need to help him. I'll be back to lock it up when you're done." Nikki returned to the counter while Cat and Millie continued sifting through the mail.

They were halfway through when Cat shoved an envelope, whose return address listed Marvin Copper, toward her.

Millie inspected the front. It was a utility bill. "Nope."

She turned her attention back to her small stack. Her pulse ticked up a notch when she found another piece of Marvin Copper's outgoing mail. "I think I've got it," she whispered.

Chapter 21

Millie quickly tucked the envelope inside her jacket.

"I guess this means I found what I was looking for, too." Cat waved the postcard in Nikki's direction. "Found it. I can lock up."

Nikki tossed the keys to Cat, who locked the mailbox before handing them back. "Thanks, Nikki. You're a doll."

The women stepped out of the atrium. They didn't stop until they reached the galley and made their way inside.

Millie pulled the envelope from her jacket pocket and handed it to Cat.

"Internal Revenue Service - Tax Court." Cat's eyes widened. "This guy has IRS issues."

"That's what I'm thinking."

293

Annette, who was on the other side of the galley, joined them. "What are you doing?"

"Snooping." Cat handed the envelope to her.

"Internal Revenue Service. Who is Marvin Copper?"

"Blackjack Blaze."

Annette held the envelope up to the light. "Are you sure?"

"I'm positive," Millie said.

"We could steam it open," Annette inspected the back of the envelope.

"Steam it open?" Cat gasped. "Isn't it illegal to tamper with US Mail?"

"I suppose it would be if we were in the United States," Annette said. "I can open this in a jiffy." She made her way across the room, and Cat hurried after her. "I don't think this is a good idea."

"No one will ever know." Annette turned the burner on high and filled an empty pot with warm water. "It's only gonna take a minute."

Cat eyed the envelope nervously. "What if someone catches us?"

"Like who?" The pot started to boil, and Annette gently waved the back of the envelope over the steam. "Almost there."

She flipped it over, gently peeled the seal open and removed the contents.

Millie leaned over Annette's shoulder. "It's a tax court hearing reminder. Looks like Blackjack aka Marvin Cooper is scheduled to show up for a hearing in less than two weeks."

"The only way he'll make this hearing is if he's planning on flying back to the States as soon as he arrives in Southampton." Annette waved the piece of paper. "This return form might not make it back to the States in two weeks, let alone Blackjack Blaze."

"Blackjack is in trouble with the IRS." Millie crossed her arms. "And he just left the country. No wonder he was in such a hurry to join Siren of the Seas, and Andy was able to hire him at the last minute."

The pieces began to fall into place. Wendy was looking for another job. Could it be she found out that Blackjack was in trouble and was trying to distance herself from him until discovering he would be working on their ship and changed her mind?

What if Wendy knew Blackjack was in trouble and threatened to turn him in to the IRS authorities? Maybe he was headed to prison for tax evasion, and she had some dirt on him so he killed her.

Millie remembered the odd comment Justin Fleming had made, how Blackjack promised to keep quiet. "It could be Justin Fleming found out about the baby, he and Wendy argued, and he pushed her over the side of the ship. Blackjack confronted him and planned to expose his identity. Fleming, in turn, knew about Blackjack's troubles with the IRS and threatened to turn him in if he did."

"That's one possible scenario," Annette agreed. "Or it could be the exact opposite with Blackjack killing Wendy because she knew about his IRS woes. Fleming, the boyfriend, found out and threatened to turn Blackjack in. Blackjack turned the tables on him, threatening to reveal him as the boyfriend if he said anything."

"We have two strong suspects, both with motive and opportunity," Millie said. "Wendy was murdered by Blackjack because of the IRS, or she was murdered by Fleming because of the baby."

Annette began folding the paper.

"Wait." Millie stopped her. "I want to snap a picture."

Cat swallowed nervously. "Patterson definitely would not approve."

"Probably not." Annette held up the piece of paper while Millie snapped a picture with her cell phone. "Speaking of Patterson, are you gonna tell him about this?"

Millie was torn. On the one hand, this was evidence. On the other, despite Annette's claims they were no longer on US soil bound by US laws, Patterson wouldn't be thrilled with the women's tactics. "Maybe."

Annette tucked the paper inside the envelope and handed it to Millie.

"I'm going to hang onto it tonight, so I can give it some thought. Either way, I think we've narrowed Wendy's killer down to two people." Millie thanked her friends and then Cat and she headed out.

Cat waited until they were in the hall. "Are you going to tell Patterson we took the mail from the box and opened it?"

"I don't know," Millie said. "What I do know is that he's not going to like it. I could leave out that part and tell him what Isla said, how Blackjack was asking a lot of questions about the outgoing mail and suggest he do what we did."

The expression on Cat's face relaxed. "That's a much better idea. You're not lying, just leaving our involvement out of it."

Millie thanked her friend for helping her and began her final rounds. As she worked, she thought about Wendy's last moments. Had the man she loved sent her hurtling over the side of the ship...or was it her boss - a man she had trusted?

Either way, it was a terrible way to go. Millie thought about the damage to the wall inside Wendy's cabin. She tried to remember if Justin's hand or Blackjack's hand was injured but couldn't. She quickly stepped off to the side and radioed Isla.

"Go ahead, Millie."

"Where are you?"

"I'm outside the comedy club."

"Hang tight. I'm coming to see you." Millie hurried down the steps and found her friend outside the club. "I have an important question."

"Sure. What?"

"When you worked with Blackjack today, did you happen to notice if his hand was injured?"

Isla thought for a moment. "You mean like bandages?"

"Possibly. It would be some sort of visible injury."

"Then the answer is no."

Millie thanked Isla and then slowly made her way home. She and Scout stepped onto the balcony. Her breath caught in her throat as she gazed at the panorama of endless stars twinkling brightly in the night sky. She shifted her gaze from the skies to the dark seas.

The cruise ship was a long way from home now. Her thoughts drifted to Fiona and then her children. If someone had told Millie a decade ago, she would be working on a cruise ship, married to the ship's captain and traveling across the ocean to another country, she would've told them they were crazy.

God had a way of turning even the most heartbreaking circumstances into the best. Over the years, Millie had learned to let go and let God handle her problems. He had never let her down.

The apartment door opened, and Nic appeared in the doorway.

"You look beat," Millie said.

"It's been a long day."

She scooped Scout up and followed Nic back inside, waiting for him to remove his shoes and jacket before they headed upstairs.

Nic eased onto the edge of the bed and pulled his socks off. "We're in for a patch of rough weather."

"How rough?"

"Rougher than I would like, but definitely not hurricane strength."

"Can't we go around it?"

"I would like to, but it's a big storm and covers a lot of area. Our best bet is to go full steam ahead and cruise through it as quickly as possible," Nic said. "I want to be on the bridge early."

"Which means it's time to turn in." Millie urged Nic to get ready first before trading places. Her husband was already fast asleep by the time she finished.

Millie eased into bed, pulling the covers up around her and began to pray. She prayed the storm would pass quickly. She prayed for her children and grandchildren. Millie also prayed for Fiona, that she would accept her.

After she finished, Millie mulled over all that had happened during the day, from uncovering Justin Fleming's identity to finding out about Blackjack's IRS woes.

Patterson would be less than thrilled to discover Millie had been snooping, but she didn't have much of a choice.

Her last thought as she drifted off to sleep was at least Amit was off the hook.

Chapter 22

Millie was up early and decided to run by the galley where she found Annette, Amit, and Danielle. A large tray of warm cinnamon rolls sat on the stainless steel counter and the aroma of cinnamon filled the air. "I didn't know there was a breakfast meeting."

"Amit and I ran into Danielle in the corridor and invited her to sample my latest recipe," Annette explained.

"They're delish. Coffee?" Danielle poured a cup from the carafe and passed it to her friend. "Annette was filling me in on yesterday's mail spy mission."

"I was thinking about something last night," Annette said. "Remember the damage to Wendy's cabin wall? We need to find out if either Blackjack or Fleming has injuries consistent with a physical confrontation."

"I already asked Isla. She said she's almost certain Blackjack isn't injured."

"I didn't notice anything either," Danielle said. "What about Fleming?"

"I wasn't paying attention. I'll mention it to Patterson, although we aren't supposed to know about the damage to the wall." Millie sighed heavily. "We did hear about Wendy's injuries, so maybe I'll mention that instead." She turned to Amit. "At least you're off the hook, my friend."

"Yes." Amit smiled. "Thank you, Miss Millie."

"You're welcome." The conversation turned to the weather, and Millie told them about the rough seas ahead.

"Thanks for the warning," Annette said. "I'll whip up an extra batch of plain broth to soothe the upset tummies."

Millie devoured her cinnamon roll and downed her coffee before consulting Andy's new scheduler. "If I leave now, I'll have just enough time to drop by

Patterson's office before heading to my Fab Abs class. I'll need it after inhaling the thousand calorie roll."

Danielle finished her treat and followed Millie to the door. "At least you don't have Adventures at Eight with Andy."

Millie eyed her friend curiously. "What is Adventures at Eight with Andy?"

"He's trying out a new morning talk show. He invited me to join him, to help field some questions from the passengers." Danielle patted her pocket. "I made my rounds yesterday, asking passengers to submit questions for the cruise director. We're televising it live on Siren of the Seas' ship channel."

"I'm going to miss it," Millie said.

"You won't miss anything. I'm sure they'll play it over and over all day long on the television."

Millie thanked Annette for the breakfast, and then Danielle and she parted ways in the corridor.

Patterson's office lights were on and the door ajar. She gave the frosted pane a light rap before poking her head around the corner.

"C'mon in, Millie." Patterson waved her in. "You're up early."

"I'm hosting a Fab Abs class coming up in a few. You got a minute?"

"Sure. Have a seat."

Millie eased into the chair across from Patterson. "I'm here to talk about Wendy Rainwell's death. You knew she was pregnant, and the baby's father is a crewmember on board the Siren of the Seas."

"I did. Blackjack Blaze told me about it when I questioned him."

"And you also knew Wendy was looking for another job," Millie said.

"Blaze mentioned that, as well. I knew he had posted a job opening online. According to him, Wendy was threatening to quit until she found out

307

he'd snagged a last minute gig on the ship. She had a change of heart, and decided to stay with Blaze in order to secure her spot on board our ship."

"Has Justin Fleming stopped by to talk to you?" Millie asked.

"He has."

"Justin Fleming was the man Cat and I photographed talking with Blackjack the other day in Bermuda." Millie shifted in her chair. "Fleming lied to Wendy. He told her his name was Jerry Dean. Blackjack lied, too, about meeting Fleming in Bermuda."

"I have the picture you sent me, but the men were too far away to confirm the identity of either of them." Patterson reached for his pen and began clicking the end. "You're sure it was Fleming and Blackjack?"

"Positive. Danielle and I caught Blackjack talking to him yesterday morning in the hall. We confronted Fleming, and he confessed to knowing

Wendy but claims he had no idea she was on board the ship until after her death, which is why I'm here. To make sure he stopped by to chat with you."

"Fleming told me he knew Wendy was looking for another job because Blaze was in the middle of an investigation."

"What kind of investigation?" Millie was almost certain he was talking about the IRS court hearing.

"You know I'm not at liberty to discuss the specifics."

On the one hand, Millie wanted to tell Patterson she knew about the IRS court hearing. On the other, she was certain he would not be thrilled with her tactics in obtaining the information.

She decided since Patterson already knew, it was best to let it go. "I know Wendy sustained some injuries - possibly prior to her fall overboard, which is the reason you suspect foul play."

It was Patterson's turn to look surprised. "Who told you that Wendy sustained injuries?"

"I have my sources. I mean, rumors go 'round."

"This is all mere speculation. I'm not going to discuss the case unless you think you have something to add."

"Only that Fleming was Wendy's lover. I'm relieved to know Amit is no longer a suspect."

"He isn't."

"And I'm sure you're taking a closer look at both Fleming and Blackjack."

"At the risk of sounding like a broken record, you know I can't talk about the case." Patterson made his way around the desk. "I appreciate you stopping by and for the heads up."

"You're welcome. If I come up with anything else, I'll let you know."

"I'm sure you will," Patterson said.

Millie's next stop was the mail drop box, to return Blackjack's IRS correspondence to the outgoing mail bin. She chatted with the woman behind the guest services desk for a few minutes before heading upstairs to begin her Fab Abs class. She had just reached the entrance when her radio squawked. "Millie, do you copy?"

"Go ahead, Isla."

"Where are you?"

"Getting ready to host an exercise class."

"Hang on. I'm right around the corner."

"10-4." Millie replaced her radio.

Isla jogged into view, her face flushed as she caught up with Millie. "Did you hear?"

"Hear what?"

"Patterson just arrested a suspect in Wendy's death."

Chapter 23

"Justin Fleming?"

"Nope. Blackjack." Isla explained she was scheduled to meet with him to go over some final details for the evening's show. Andy met her at the door and told her Blackjack wouldn't be performing.

"Patterson must've gotten his hands on some sort of evidence or information linking Blackjack to Wendy's death."

"I always thought the guy was on the sketchy side," Isla said.

Millie thanked her for the information and joined the instructor and the attendees. As she stretched, she thought about Justin and Blackjack. Maybe Blackjack was fleeing the country in an attempt to skip out on his IRS hearing. Wendy found out about it and planned to turn him in...after she met up with Jerry aka Justin.

Justin wasn't exactly innocent, either. At the very least, he lied to Wendy about his identity and had no plans to confess to the authorities that he was the man involved with Wendy. Both of them had something to hide, but was it enough to motivate one of them to commit murder?

There was still the lingering issue of the damage to Wendy's cabin. Surely, Patterson would be anxious to determine if someone had confronted or attacked the woman.

Something about the death was off. The more Millie thought about it, the more she was convinced Blackjack wasn't responsible for Wendy's death. He could've easily fired her and then boarded the ship.

There was also the mark on Wendy's neck that Sharky had mentioned. It could be she sustained her injury while going overboard if she clipped the side of the ship, but there was also the possibility that something...or someone else had caused it.

The class ended, and she decided to swing by the kitchen, to fill Annette and Amit in on Blackjack's detainment. The galley was a madhouse. She had turned to go when her friend spotted her and waved her over. "You heard?"

"About Patterson detaining Blackjack?"

"One of the regular pizza and deli workers was in here earlier talking about it. Now that I had a positive ID, I asked the guy about Fleming. He said he's taking Wendy's death hard."

Millie wrinkled her nose. "He didn't seem too broken up about it when Danielle and I confronted him."

Annette shrugged. "Delayed reaction? People handle death differently. Donovan Sweeney sent him downstairs to work in the crew galley until further notice. I guess he was causing a commotion last night during his shift and passengers complained about it."

"I have to admit I'm surprised. I was under the impression he couldn't care less what happened to Wendy. She didn't even know his real name."

One of the kitchen crewmembers stepped over to ask Annette a question and Millie excused herself.

Perhaps Fleming was taking her death hard...finally after several days. Or maybe it was all an act, and now that he'd been found out, he was pretending to be the mourning boyfriend.

It was early in the afternoon when Millie began to notice the ship rolling and a scarcity of passengers. There were several loud rumbles of thunder, flashes of lightning and then the skies opened up.

Millie hovered near the doors leading to the lido deck and watched as the drenched crewmembers scrambled to secure the lounge chairs, which were sliding across the open deck.

The crewmembers finally gave up and joined her inside. "It's getting nasty out there."

"Yes, it is a bad storm," one of the men agreed.

The next couple of hours were rough, and Millie began to feel queasy. With a quick stop for some saltine crackers and ginger ale, she was back on track.

Slowly, the ship's rocking lessened, and the skies grew brighter. She let out a sigh of relief. The storm finally passed in the early evening, just in time for Millie's break.

Anxious to avoid the crowds and on the off chance she might run into Justin Fleming, Millie ran down to the crew dining room to grab a quick bite to eat.

She radioed Danielle, and invited her to join her. To her surprise, both Danielle and Isla showed up a short time later.

The women filled their plates with food and joined Millie at the table. She waited until they were seated. "All three of us with a dinner break at the same time is unheard of."

"You can blame it on Blackjack's fiasco." Danielle set her food on the table and the tray on an empty chair. "Andy is fit to be tied."

"No kidding." Isla reached for her fork. "He's running around like a chicken with his head cut off."

"Poor Andy. I figured he would easily come up with a backup plan."

"Even his fancy new scheduler can't save him from this catastrophe," Isla quipped.

"According to Annette, Justin Fleming is taking Wendy's death hard," Millie said. "Donovan transferred him down here to work in the crew dining room because he was upsetting the passengers."

"I feel sorry for him," Isla sympathized. "He had no idea she was on board the ship or pregnant."

"He didn't seem too upset about it when Millie and I confronted him," Danielle said.

"I thought the same thing." Millie stabbed a tomato slice with her fork. "I guess everyone handles grief differently. He's probably around here somewhere. He works the night shift."

The discussion turned to the rough seas and storms earlier in the day. The trio compared notes, all agreeing many of the passengers must have decided to hunker down inside their cabins to ride out the storm.

Now that the worst of it was behind them, they would be anxious to escape their cabins and join in the activities.

"We'll be hopping the rest of this evening," Millie predicted.

"I would rather be busy." Isla finished off the last of her chicken noodle soup and eyed the buffet area. "I was thinking of maybe snagging a piece of chocolate pie. Anyone care to join me?"

"I wouldn't mind seeing what's up there." Millie placed her napkin next to her plate, and she and Isla made a beeline for the dessert counter.

"I've been trying to eat healthier lately," Millie said. "Maybe I'll have a small dish of ice cream."

She let several of the galley crewmembers pass by before reaching for an ice cream bowl. One of them, a young woman, began transferring plates of cherry cobbler to the dessert section. There was a large bandage on the woman's right hand. "That looks like a doozy."

"It's not too bad." The woman finished placing the small plates in the cooler section. "I've had worse."

"The kitchen can be a dangerous place." Millie filled her small bowl before returning to the table.

Danielle patted her stomach as she eyed the chocolate and vanilla swirl. "Ice cream sounds good. I changed my mind. I think I'll have some, too."

The friends finished eating their desserts and carried their dirty dishes to the bin by the door before stepping into the hallway.

Millie paused to check her schedule. "I'm off for another half hour. What's on your agenda?"

"The usual...Mix and Mingles," Danielle sighed.

"Piano bar singalong," Isla reported. "I should switch with you, Danielle. I can't carry a tune. It's embarrassing."

"I hate Mix and Mingles. They're boring."

Millie thought about the Senior Mix and Mingles and Thomas Windsor's recent attack. "The one I hosted the other day was the complete opposite. Thomas Windsor had a gang of women ticked at him."

"Sounds about right," Danielle chuckled.

The women began walking down the corridor, shifting to the right to let a group of crewmembers pass.

Millie did a double take when she realized one of them looked familiar. It was Justin Fleming. He either didn't notice her or just didn't acknowledge her.

She thought about stopping to offer her condolences, but it was too late. He and the other crewmembers had already made their way past and disappeared inside the crew dining area.

"Did you see that?" Danielle had noticed, too. "Fleming passed us looking none too happy."

"I thought the same thing." Millie did an about face and headed back to the galley. She inched toward the door and peered through the glass pane.

Millie watched as Fleming grabbed an apron from the rack. He slipped it over his head and crossed to the other side of the dining room. The woman Millie had spoken with earlier met him near the back bar area.

Millie studied his face and then shifted her gaze to the woman's bandaged hand. "I...will you look at that?"

Chapter 24

Millie motioned for Danielle and Isla to join her. "Fleming is fighting with a woman."

They watched as the young woman jabbed her finger at him. She spun on her heel and started to walk away.

Fleming grabbed her arm and jerked her back.

Millie saw the woman raise her hand, as if she was going to hit him, and then stop. There were more words exchanged before the woman stomped off.

Fleming watched her go before slowly following behind.

"Who is she?" Millie nudged Isla's arm. "Isla, I need the name of the woman with the bandaged hand."

"Why?"

"I'll explain later." She opened the dining room door and propelled her friend forward. "She's wearing a nametag. It should be a piece of cake."

Millie watched Isla approach the counter. "Danielle, think about the damage to Wendy's cabin, the hole in the wall. As far as we know, Blackjack isn't injured, and neither is Fleming. I just checked."

"This mystery woman, the one who argued with Fleming, is injured."

"What if we were wrong? What if this woman is or was Fleming's girlfriend, she found out about Wendy and the baby, and there was some sort of confrontation? The woman managed to lure Wendy onto the upper deck and then pushed her over the side."

"If that's the case and something happened inside Wendy's cabin, I still don't understand why she never reported it," Danielle said.

"Unless the altercation happened a short time before she went overboard. She planned to, but for some reason never made it that far."

Isla joined them moments later. "Her name is Aliyah Persimon."

"Aliyah Persimon," Millie repeated the name. "We need to find out more about her."

"Cat," Millie and Danielle said in unison.

Millie stepped off to the side and dialed Cat's cell phone.

"Hey, Millie."

"Hey, Cat. I need the 411 on someone." Millie rattled off the woman's name.

"It will take a couple of minutes to pull up her information." There was a clicking sound on the other end. "She works nights in the crew dining room and galley."

Millie had a sudden thought. "What about store purchases? Has she made any recent purchases like bandages?"

"Yeah." There were more tapping sounds on the other end. "Her most recent purchase was a box of gauze bandages, hydrogen peroxide, some rubbing alcohol and a tube of antibiotic cream."

Millie's heart skipped a beat. "Can you tell me when Aliyah purchased those items?"

"Sure. They were purchased at nine o'clock on Sunday morning, right after we opened."

"One more question."

"Fire away."

"Were you working Sunday morning and if so, do you remember Aliyah?"

Cat was quiet. "I was working, but I don't remember her. So many people pass through here every day it's hard to remember anyone unless they're complaining or trying to return something."

"I'm sure." Millie thanked Cat for the information and disconnected the call. "Aliyah purchased bandages, hydrogen peroxide, rubbing alcohol and antibiotic cream from Ocean Treasures Sunday morning."

Danielle's jaw dropped. "Only hours after Wendy went overboard."

"Patterson needs to hear about this."

Isla returned to work while Danielle and Millie headed to the security office. Patterson wasn't in, but Oscar, his right-hand man, was able to track him down.

He agreed to meet them in the atrium and was already there when the women arrived.

"Can we talk somewhere private, maybe out on the open deck?" Millie asked.

"Sure." Patterson headed to the nearest exit, and Millie and Danielle trailed behind.

Millie waited until they were alone. "We discovered something very interesting. We believe one of Justin Fleming's acquaintances, friends, whatever, may have been involved in Wendy's death."

"Acquaintance?" Patterson asked. "A close acquaintance?"

"We caught him arguing with a woman in the crew dining room just now. Her name is Aliyah Persimon." Millie rambled on about Aliyah's injury, her call to Cat, and their discovery that Aliyah had purchased items for her injured hand only hours after Wendy's death.

Patterson's jaw tightened. "You're sure."

"You can verify the information yourself. What if Aliyah and Justin were an item and she found out about Wendy? Aliyah confronted Wendy and they fought inside her cabin..."

Patterson held up a hand. "Wait a minute. Who said anyone fought inside Wendy's cabin?"

Millie clasped her hands. "I...can't reveal my sources, but I believe an argument may have taken place inside Wendy's cabin shortly before her death."

"We'll delve into that later," Patterson promised. "Continue."

"So Wendy and her killer fought inside her cabin. Somehow, Wendy was lured upstairs and onto an open deck where her killer pushed her overboard."

"And you think it may have been Aliyah Persimon," Patterson said.

"It's possible," Millie admitted. "I think it's worth taking a closer look."

"I will." He wagged his finger at Millie. "We'll discuss your 'sources' later."

Danielle waited until Patterson had walked away. "You're in hot water."

"Like that's anything new," Millie groaned.

*****

Millie hoped to hear some news about Aliyah Persimon, but the evening wore on, and there wasn't a peep. She even stopped to chat with Annette, to see if she or Amit had heard anything, but as far as they knew, there wasn't even a whisper of rumor about a new suspect in Wendy's death.

Millie went to bed that night, wondering if Blackjack was still in the holding cell or if Patterson had even bothered to follow up on her lead.

The couple was up early the next morning and hit the ground running.

Millie was beginning to suspect Patterson hadn't bothered following up on her suspicions until later that evening when Blackjack Blaze showed up at Andy's office while she was there.

Even Andy was surprised. He did a double take before springing from his chair. "Blaze. You're out."

"Yes. Dave Patterson finally did his job and figured out what happened to Wendy." He shot Millie a sideways glance. "I'm not sure if I'm at liberty to discuss the specifics with mixed company."

"I'm not mixed company." Millie gave him an exasperated look. "I may know more about the case than you do. Let me guess...Patterson is detaining a woman in connection with Wendy's death."

A flicker of surprise crossed the man's face. "As a matter of fact, he did."

"It was Justin Fleming's girlfriend, Aliyah Persimon."

"No one is supposed to know this," Blackjack replied. "Patterson will be furious if he finds out the information is floating around."

"It's not floating around." Millie tapped the side of her forehead. "I'm the one who gave Patterson Aliyah's name."

"You?" Blackjack snorted. "What do you know about murder investigations?"

"A lot more than she should," Andy groaned.

"Well." Blackjack tugged on the bottom of his jacket. "I'm here to be reinstated with my evening show now that my name has been cleared."

"Of course. We can add you tonight."

"I'll need a new assistant. Isla was okay, but a little sloppy."

Andy slowly shifted his gaze to Millie, but she was already shaking her head. "No way. I refuse. In fact..." She scrambled to her feet. "I need to get back to work."

She didn't see Blackjack again, and Andy never paged her to meet him in his office. Millie caught the tail end of Sea-Fi's early show, and was thrilled to discover that Felix was Blackjack's new assistant.

Felix added an extra element of humor and charm. After it ended, Millie decided her feisty friend was Blackjack's ideal sidekick.

Despite Patterson's attempts to keep the news of Wendy's investigation and the arrest of Aliyah under wraps, the ship's crew was abuzz at the unexpected turn in events.

Millie learned from Annette that Justin Fleming, although not charged in Wendy's death, was terminated on the grounds of lying to the authorities regarding his relationship with both women.

Since all of what Millie heard was mere speculation, she figured she would get the facts from a reliable source...Nic.

The ship docked at the Port of Ponta Delgada early the next morning. She'd decided Nic and she would check out the Sete Cidades and sample some of the local cuisine after the tour.

Millie learned from her research that the Sete Cidades, an extinct volcano, was one of the Seven Natural Wonders of Portugal. It was nicknamed 'seven cities' because of the seven peaks surrounding the lakes.

The couple exited the ship early to meet their guide near the end of the pier. Millie enjoyed the scenic drive to the Cidades, and before she knew it, they had reached Vista do Rei, the rim of the crater overlooking a tiny parish.

Their guide pulled the vehicle onto the side of the road and shifted into park. "Go explore. I will meet you back here in an hour."

Nic held the door for his wife and then they stepped over to a viewing area. In the middle of the volcanic crater were twin lakes, separated by a man-made bridge. The smaller of the two lakes was a vivid green.

Millie studied her brochure. "Lagoa Verde or Green Lake."

She shifted her gaze and peered at the larger of the two lakes, a deep blue and named Lagoa Azul or Blue Lake. "The view is absolutely breathtaking."

"What's that?" Nic motioned to a wooden sign with an arrow pointing down a sloped path.

"Adventure Ahead. I wonder what kind of adventure." Intrigued, he followed the path and his wife reluctantly trailed behind.

It led to a clearing and a large platform. A trio of people stood near the base talking to a man who was securing a safety harness. "It's a zip line," Nic said. "That looks like fun."

"No way." Millie stubbornly shook her head. "The Segways on St. Kitts is the top of my max excitement level."

"But you took a zip line in Grand Turk." Nic watched as the man catapulted off the platform and disappeared from sight.

"If you'll recall, it wasn't by choice."

"You love excitement."

"I do, just not a pulse-thumping, heart-pumping as I pass out on my way down the side of a mountain thrill ride." She could see the look of disappointment on her husband's face. "Tell you what…I'll think about it. Maybe someday," Millie said. "Just not today."

The couple retraced their steps back to the main lookout and posed for several pictures. Too soon, their time ended and they reluctantly returned to the van.

During the return trip, the guide recommended a market not far from the ship and a street vendor where they could sample the local cuisine.

The couple had no trouble finding the vendor. The menu was limited to a half dozen sandwich choices, made fresh and delivered to their makeshift table, which consisted of three large, wooden crates.

"Thank you for going along with my idea to visit the Cidades," Millie said after they were seated.

"You're welcome. I enjoyed the tour. The mountains were beautiful." Nic lifted his sandwich. "To a taste of the island and a perfect way to end our day in paradise."

"A perfect day," Millie agreed. "I'm guessing the authorities were waiting first thing this morning to escort Aliyah Persimon off the ship where she'll be flown back to the United States."

Nic sobered. "She was. Aliyah found out about Wendy and the baby and discovered the baby's father was her boyfriend, Justin Fleming."

According to Nic, Aliyah confronted Wendy. She somehow tricked her into meeting her on an upper open deck, where she pushed her over the side of the ship. "Patterson reviewed the surveillance cameras a second time and caught Aliyah walking midship deck twelve and in the direction of the area where Wendy went over, not long before the incident took place."

Millie interrupted. "What about the damage to Wendy's cabin wall?"

"Inconclusive," Nic said. "Aliyah swears she never confronted Wendy inside her cabin, so your snooping around was a waste of time."

"Maybe. Maybe not. You said 'inconclusive.' What about the mark on Wendy's neck and her cause of death?"

"Preliminary autopsy report is that Wendy drowned. The marks on her neck may have been caused by Aliyah or from some other source."

"And the injuries to Aliyah's hand?" Millie prompted.

"They're deep scratches. Aliyah admitted she fought with Wendy before the fall and that Wendy scratched her."

"I'm sure she was fighting desperately for her life." Millie switched gears. "What about Fleming?"

"He swears he wasn't even aware Wendy was on board until after her death, and he's willing to testify under oath, as well as take a lie detector test."

"So Justin, although a cheat and womanizer, wasn't a killer." Millie had another thought. "What about Blackjack's IRS woes?"

"I don't know. Donovan Sweeney is looking into it." Nic reached for his napkin. "We'll be in Southampton before you know it. Perhaps we can slip in a partial day off to explore the city."

A look of concern clouded Millie's face.

"What's wrong? You don't want to see Southampton?"

"I do. It's Sharky."

"Sharky Kiveski?"

"Yes. He met a Russian woman online. He sent her money and plans to meet her in Southampton the day we arrive." Millie twirled her drink straw. "I'm getting a bad feeling about her. What if it's a scam?"

"He's a grown man," Nic said. "I'm sure he can handle himself."

"Right." Millie knew her husband was right, but she still vowed to have a talk with Sharky before they reached the port.

She was also concerned about Annette's upcoming doctor appointment and planned to mention it again in case her friend wanted someone to go with her.

The couple finished their light lunch and then hitched a ride on the city bus back to the port.

Millie slowed as they approached the security gate. "We need pictures to record our memories." She snapped several selfies, and then Nic stood off to the side patiently waiting for his wife to take pictures of the city.

"Are you ready to go home?"

"I am." Millie slowly gazed at her surroundings. It was the last time her feet would be on solid ground before stepping off the ship in Southampton. "I'm ready to embark on the next leg of our adventure."

The end.

If you enjoyed reading "Transatlantic Tragedy," please take a moment to leave a review. It would mean so much to me. Thank you! -Hope Callaghan

The series continues...Cruise Ship Cozy Mysteries Book 17 Coming Soon!

Books in This Series

Starboard Secrets: Book 1
Portside Peril: Book 2
Lethal Lobster: Book 3
Deadly Deception: Book 4
Vanishing Vacationers: Book 5
Cruise Control: Book 6
Killer Karaoke: Book 7
Suite Revenge: Book 8
Cruisin' for a Bruisin': Book 9
High Seas Heist: Book 10
Family, Friends and Foes: Book 11:
Murder on Main: Book 12
Fatal Flirtation: Book 13
Deadly Delivery: Book 14
Reindeer & Robberies: Book 15
Transatlantic Tragedy: Book 16
Book 17: Coming Soon!
Cruise Ship Cozy Mysteries Box Set I (Books 1-3)
Cruise Ship Cozy Mysteries Box Set II (Books 4-6)
Cruise Ship Cozy Mysteries Box Set III (Books 7-9)

Friendship Bread Starter Original Recipe

Ingredients:

1 - .25 ounce package active dry yeast

1/4 cup warm water (100 degrees F / 45 degrees C)

3 cups all-purpose flour, divided

3 cups white sugar, divided

3 cups milk

Directions:

-In a small bowl, dissolve yeast in water. Let stand 10 minutes. In a 2-quart container glass, plastic or ceramic container, combine 1 cup flour and 1 cup sugar. Mix thoroughly or flour will lump when milk is added. Slowly stir in 1 cup milk and dissolved yeast mixture. Cover loosely and let stand until bubbly. **Consider this day 1 of the ten-day cycle.** Leave loosely covered at room temperature.

343

-On days 2 through 4; stir starter with a spoon. Day 5; stir in 1 cup flour, 1 cup sugar and 1 cup milk. Days 6 through 9; stir only.

-Day 10; stir in 1 cup flour, 1 cup sugar and 1 cup milk. Remove 1 cup to make your first bread, give 2 cups to friends along with this recipe, and your favorite Bread recipe. Store the remaining 1 cup starter in a container in the refrigerator, or begin the 10 day process over again (beginning with step 2).

Notes:

*Do not use metal pans or metal utensils.

*Once you have made the starter, you will consider it Day One, and thus ignore step 1 in this recipe and proceed with step 2. You can also freeze this starter in 1 cup measures for later use. Frozen starter will take at least 3 hours at room temperature to thaw before using.

Friendship Bread – Final Baking Instructions

(The "original" starter recipe)

Ingredients:

1 cup Friendship Bread Starter (see recipe above)

2/3 cup vegetable oil

3 eggs

2 cups all-purpose flour

1 cup white sugar

1 teaspoon ground cinnamon

1/2 teaspoon salt

1/2 teaspoon baking soda

1 1/4 teaspoons baking powder

1 teaspoon vanilla extract

*See below to personalize

Directions:

-Preheat oven to 350 degrees F (175 degrees C).

Grease 2 (9x5 inch) loaf pans.

-In a large bowl, combine the bread starter with oil, eggs, 2 cups flour, 1 cup sugar, 1 teaspoon ground cinnamon, 1/2 teaspoon salt, 1/2 teaspoon baking soda, 1 1/4 teaspoons baking powder, and 1 teaspoon vanilla. Mix well. Pour into prepared loaf pans.

-Bake in preheated oven for 50 to 60 minutes.

*There are two suggested variations:

Add: 1 cup white chocolate chips, 1 cup macadamia nuts (chopped), 1 box of white chocolate pudding before baking.

Add: 1 cup of craisins (dried cranberries), 1 cup of walnuts, and 1 box of vanilla pudding.

1 smashed banana, 1 cup of walnuts, and 1 box of banana cream pudding before baking.

Cinnamon Bread Recipe

(Courtesy of Wanda Downs)

Ingredients: (batter)

1 cup butter, softened

2 cups white sugar

2 eggs

2 cups buttermilk or homemade buttermilk (2 cups
milk plus 2 tablespoons vinegar or lemon juice

4 cups flour

2 teaspoons baking soda

Cinnamon swirl:

2/3 cups brown sugar

2 teaspoons cinnamon

Directions:

Preheat oven to 350 degrees.

Cream together butter, 2 cups white sugar and eggs.

Add milk, flour and baking soda.

Grease two loaf pans.

Pour 1/4 of batter into each pan (reserving approximately half the batter).

Sprinkle 1/3 of cinnamon mixture on top of each 1/2 batter.

Add remaining batter to pans.

Sprinkle remaining cinnamon mixture evenly over the top of each load pan.

Swirl with knife.

Bake at 350 degrees for 45-50 minutes, or until toothpick comes out clean.

Let cool for 20 minutes before removing from pan.